The Lost Frost Girl

The Lost Frost Girl

Amy Wilson

Katherine Tegen Books
An Imprint of HarperCollinsPublishers

HarperCollins Publishers
Since 1817

Katherine Tegen Books is an imprint of HarperCollins Publishers.

The Lost Frost Girl
 For information address HarperCollins Children's Books, a division of HarperCollins Publishers, 195 Broadway, New York, NY 10007.
www.harpercollinschildrens.com

Library of Congress Control Number 2017943386
ISBN 978-0-06-267148-6

Typography by Heather Daugherty
17 18 19 20 21 CG/LSCH 10 9 8 7 6 5 4 3 2 1
❄
First Edition
First published 2017 in the United Kingdom by Macmillan Children's Books, an imprint of Pan Macmillan

This book set in 12-point Stempel Garamond.

For Lee

Jack

I thought I saw a figure there,
Dancing at the lake,
Alone but for the tide of ice
That followed in his wake.

I thought I saw a shadow there,
In winter's cruelest hour,
When frost spills, wicked beautiful,
Upon the boldest flower.

I thought I saw you there, Jack Frost,
I blinked and you were gone.
The magic that you left behind
Now sparkling in the dawn.

Part One

1

When you have a kid, don't call it something stupid.

Don't call it Apple, or Pear, or Mung Bean.

Don't call it Owl.

This advice is a bit late for me. Because she did. She did call me Owl. Twelve years ago she looked down at a tiny little baby—me—and decided that Owl would be a good way to go.

I guess she didn't know then that I would grow up to have white-blond hair that flicks around my face like feathers, no matter what I do with it. That my eyes would turn from baby blue to the palest brown, almost yellow. That my nose would be on the beaky side.

She should have seen that last one coming, though. I inherited it from her.

I like owls. I think they're beautiful. But you know, my head doesn't rotate 360 degrees. I can't fly. I don't hunt at night.

All these are questions the other kids have asked me over the years. Mom laughs when I tell her.

"See!" she cries, looking up from whatever she's doing, a glint in her dark eyes. "Already you stand out from the crowd. Already you are different. Isn't it a wonderful thing?"

She's beautiful, my mom. Not in a subjective way, like she's my mom therefore she must be beautiful. She's actually beautiful. She has these big dark eyes, masses of dark hair, and when she smiles, when she laughs, it's very difficult not to join in.

I do try my very best not to join in.

Her name is Isolde. She wears lots of bright colors and tinkling bangles on her wrists. She smells of warm things: vanilla, cinnamon, oranges, and black currants, and something deeper that's just her, I guess.

My friends love her.

Which is annoying.

"Owl McBride!"

I look up from my desk. Mr. Leonard is perched on the edge of his table, his ankles crossed in front of him. His hands rest on the table, one finger tap-tapping against it. There's a diagram on the board behind him, but it's all squiggles to me.

"Are you concentrating?"

"Yes, sir."

"On the lesson, I mean, as opposed to your doodling?"

I blush as a roll of laughter goes around the room.

"Yes, sir. Sorry, sir."

"That's all right. If you can tell me what *pi* is."

Clearly it'd be a bad idea to tell him it's something I eat for dessert. His eyebrows are just daring me to do it. They look like black marker pen stripes, drawn too high on his forehead, trying to hide beneath his shaggy dark hair.

"It's where the circle has a diameter and the circumference is . . . when you calculate it . . . that's *pi.*"

I smile hopefully, but Mr. Leonard drops his head and sighs.

"I suppose," he says, standing up and walking to the board. "I suppose I should just be happy that you know the right words!"

He starts jabbing at the board with a blue marker, making more squiggles. I copy them down in my book. The rest of the class does the same. Mallory, next to me, is still laughing.

"Shh!" I hiss at her, my pen moving across the paper, making alien mathematical shapes I've no use for.

❄❄❄

It was an owl. The doodle in my math book. I draw them, over and over. Little ones, big ones, owls with crazy whirly eyes, owls swooping from the sky. They're in all the borders of my lined schoolbooks. They're on Post-it notes around my bedroom. I have sketches of them, paintings, even little clay figures.

I'm not saying they're good. Actually, if you walked into my bedroom you'd probably run back out again screaming. They're a bit intense.

Mom loves them. *Loves* them. She thinks it's me expressing myself.

Drawing myself, over and over again.

Mallory just rolls her eyes when she sees a new one now. She bought me a card with a puffin on it for my birthday a couple of weeks ago.

"Maybe a change?" she wrote inside. "Now that you're twelve?"

But I'm not *called* Puffin.

And there has to be a reason.

A reason Mom called me Owl.

2

Clearly I must have a father somewhere. Everybody has one, after all.

But Mom won't tell me who he is. There are no photos, no certificates with his name on them. Nothing. And whenever I ask her she goes all misty-eyed and tells me he was a beautiful man who left her a beautiful gift. She wanders off to see him in her imagination and leaves me behind, in the kitchen, for example, while dinner starts to burn.

When I was younger, she would tell me fairy tales about how they met in one of the magical wintry lands from her old storybook, and I loved them, because it *was* magical, and I was just a kid. But I got older and it started to annoy me, because I wasn't a kid anymore, and I wanted real answers.

So she stopped with the stories and got vague instead. And that's the source of most of our arguments.

That and the Owl thing.

It's nearly impossible to have a satisfying argument with my mom. She watches seriously while you make your initial point. She considers, nodding, and then tells you something completely pointless.

"Dear sweet child," she says now, deflecting my latest attempt to ask about fatherly things as I untangle myself from my scarf after school. "Some things are not supposed to wear labels or names. Some things remain a mystery, however hard we butt up against them. . . ." She smiles, pouring jasmine tea into two tiny china cups. She pushes one along the kitchen counter to me.

"So you don't know who he is, then?"

"Oh, I know him," she says, picking up her own cup and looking down at the steaming amber liquid. "I've told you about him, Owl, you just never believed me. . . ."

"Well if you know him, he must have a name," I say. "And you can give it to me. Can't you?"

She takes a sip.

"Owl, drink!" she says when she's finished. "It's only good when it's hot."

I take a sip.

"I have nothing to give you except this moment," she says then. "That is all there is. You and me, in this kitchen, drinking our tea."

The china cups have jade green dragons inside them, eternally chasing their tails around the white background, breathing fire at themselves.

Sometimes I feel a bit like those dragons.

"Who needs a dad, anyway?" sighs Mallory on the phone later, when I tell her of my latest failed attempt.

That's easy for her to say. Hers is probably outside cleaning the car right now. I look out of the window, as if mine might just be there, looking for me, waiting for me to notice him. Brittle autumn leaves fall from the trees on the street and a little shiver runs down my spine—mid-November, and winter is here. Soon there will be frost and ice sweeping over the rooftops, curling down trees, making the gray pavements sparkle. The thought makes my skin itch, makes me impatient. The need to know where I come from is almost overwhelming.

". . . and flipping annoying," Mallory's voice cuts in. "Honestly, you don't need a dad, Owl."

"I do," I tell her firmly. "At least his name . . ."

"You are a bit fixated on names."

"And why do you think that is?"

"Mallory isn't all that, you know. It means unlucky, for goodness sake."

That's true enough. But it's better than Owl.

We spend the rest of the conversation talking about Justin. Mallory talks a lot about Justin. She's convinced they're soulmates, even though he's going out with Daisy.

"English tomorrow," she says as we say our goodbyes. "A whole hour of English . . ."

Which means sharing a class with Justin. Which means they'll compete with each other every time a question is asked and try to answer it in the most complicated, literary way possible, and I just have to sit there and watch it all and feel a bit stupid. I usually have a couple of new owls by the time I come out of English lessons.

I chuck the phone onto my bed with a huff and go to the window, muttering to the carved owl on the bedpost about how boys complicate everything. As I watch, half distracted, something moves between the trees outside the apartment, something lean and hunched, with spidery limbs—something so alien, so out of place, that my skin tightens with fear before I've even worked out what it is. I lean closer to get a better look, my breath misting the glass, but all I can see is shadows.

I have a good imagination. It was probably just a raccoon. I pull the curtains with a sharp tug and tell myself off for being such a kid.

About the legends Mom used to tell me. She hasn't got that old book out for years now, and I sort of miss it. I'd never admit it, but when I struggle to get to sleep sometimes I imagine the stories were true, and my father really is from some great fantasy land. I remember the way her voice changed as she told me of those strange places, the way her eyes glazed as she spoke of fairies and sprites, talking trees and fearsome queens. Sometimes it was a little scary—as if I'd lost her to that other world.

3

THE WORLD OF WINTER

It was ever winter there. The deepest, coldest, the bluest winter. The winter of the world. The sky changed as day turned to night and night to day once more, but the sun was a cold white disk in the sky, and the moon shone brighter against the darkness, but still there was no heat about it.

Her ears screamed with the dead silence in the air.

Her chest burned to breathe against the bitter of the wind.

He found her in the clearing between the trees that towered out in every direction: black with bark and white with frost. He found her by the plume of her breath, by the snap of frozen twigs beneath her boots as she turned and turned and turned again, waiting for something to become familiar.

Nothing was familiar.

He was blue white as if he'd never seen the summertime. His eyes were mirrors in the dawn and his dark hair was tipped with the frost of the land. When he reached out his hand she thought it would be like ice.

It was not.

He gestured back the way he'd come and his grip tightened. She breathed in and prepared to launch her questions at him, but even as her lips gathered he shook his head and put a finger to her mouth.

"Not here, not now."

"But why am I here and what is this place and who are you and where is home and where am I and who are you?"

He considered her and took his hands away, and she was colder than she had ever been and clung to herself, but he was quick to unclasp his robe and sweep it over her shoulders.

Once more he took her hand.

"Now?"

"Now we run."

The cloak he'd drawn around her was charcoal gray and heavy. It was the rough-smooth of new wool and though the clearing was freezing and the wind howled in her ears she was not cold.

4

There's a new boy in homeroom the next morning. His name is Avery. He has tawny-brown hair in a long braid snaking down his back.

Mr. Varley looked at Avery for a long time when he first walked in, his mouth twitching as though he wanted to tell him to go and cut it off immediately.

We'd all stopped talking and were waiting to see what would happen. And then Mr. Varley nodded and turned back to the class.

"CLASS!" he roared. "This is Avery!"

He loves to roar, Mr. Varley. I'm glad I only have him for homeroom in the morning. I think a whole lesson would probably give me a heart attack. The good thing about it is that if he's yelling at you for being late nobody really listens.

Avery is in my geography class. He follows me in and strides past me to the back of the room and sits in the far corner by the window. I sit in my usual seat, across from his, and watch as everyone else comes in and takes a second to work out where they're going to sit, now that he's interrupted the flow.

He's getting some evil looks from the boys, especially Conor.

Conor is one of those boys who can be really nice when it's just him, and an absolute idiot when he's surrounded by his friends. He likes things to have an order, likes to be on top of it all.

Avery, sitting where Conor normally sits and the general air of swagger about him, is definitely putting a wrench in the works.

It's a great start to the lesson.

He has the strangest copper-colored eyes, and I don't know whether it's because he's sitting by the window, but they're shining like beacons as he looks at me.

And he keeps looking at me.

And to start with, it was a good feeling, but now I don't know where to look or what to do, and my new owl has grown a braid.

It's not a good look on an owl.

5

"What is it with the new guy?" Mallory falls in next to me as I head for science, jostling in close so she can whisper. "Do you know him from somewhere?"

"No!"

She looks back over her shoulder. "He's a bit intense, isn't he? He's, like, actively *not* staring at you now. . . ."

"I'm ignoring him."

"You're blushing!"

I lower my head, grabbing her arm. My skin is prickling with all the unwanted attention.

"Ouch! Where have you been? You're freezing!"

I pull my hand away from her and look down at my fingers. Other kids barge past me, but I barely notice them, because my skin is blue white and sparkling beneath the fluorescent lights as if someone just painted the back of my hands with frost. I flex my fingers and the prickling sensation intensifies, my forearms tingling beneath my sweater.

"What *is* that?" Mallory whispers, leaning closer. I whip my hands away and shove them deep into my pockets.

"Nothing!"

What was it?

"Come on, we'll be late." I hustle Mallory along to science, avoiding her eyes and telling myself blue fingers are perfectly normal.

"What is up with you?" Mallory asks as we walk home later. She stares at me. "You've hardly said a word this whole way—are you coming down with something? Your hands were *so* cold earlier."

"I'm okay. The new boy was a bit freaky. . . ."

"That's boys though, isn't it? They're all a bit freaky. Justin was giving me eyes today, even though he was walking along holding hands with Daisy."

"Ugh. And you still like him?"

"The heart wants what the heart wants," she says in an awful sappy voice, fluttering her eyelashes at me.

"You're terrible."

She laughs and starts telling me about how noble she really is, and how she'd never *do* anything because she'd never be able to live with herself. The sun is low in the sky and our breath plumes out in front of us. It was the first frost of winter this morning and it's still bitterly cold, everything covered with a low silver mist. I look down at my hands. I can't forget what that felt like, what it looked like. What *was* it?

"I know what this is all about," Mallory says suddenly, making me jump.

"What?" I fold my arms, pushing my hands out of sight as she peers at me.

"Your dad! I know it's been getting to you. . . . You should just ask your mom, have it out with her once and for all." She tucks her arm through mine.

I dig my hands into my pockets. "I have!"

"But have you really? Like, properly looked her in the face and asked for a name, straight out? Told her you won't budge until you know what it is?"

She might have a point there. But we don't get to talk any more about it, because Conor and his friends catch up with us and put an end to all sensible conversation.

Mom's in full-on sketchy mode when I get in. Literally. She's up in the attic studio, pale dusk streaming in through the skylight, sketching winter scenes on enormous sheets of paper. Mountains and deep valleys where single houses nestle between towering, skeletal trees—frozen waterfalls and solitary eagles high above tangled forests. It's a new commission. I didn't really listen to the details, but she's lost to it, so I don't ask her about fathers. If I asked her now she'd tell me more stories, I can see by the sparkle in her eye when she looks up.

"Owl! My love, did you have a good day?"

I nod, dropping my bag on the wooden, paint-splattered floor.

"I made soup!" she says, as if it just came to her. "Let me finish here and we'll eat. . . . Do you have any homework?"

"Yesss." I sigh, getting out my math books. I have my own desk up here, next to hers. I sit opposite her, notice a few gray hairs among all the black as she lowers her head to her work. She's got a pencil behind one ear and a smudge of charcoal on her cheek, and she must have dressed in a hurry: her sweater is inside out. I watch her sketch for a while. There's something magical about the way it all emerges. Clever hands. I look down at my own. They're the same shape as hers. Broad palm, long fingers.

I need to ask her. Mallory's right—I need to *know.*

"Mom?"

"Hmm?"

She doesn't look up. I take a deep breath, but I don't know where to begin. My chest tightens as I imagine the words coming out, tangling as I try to make her understand. I've asked so many times, and she's never given me a real answer. How can I convince her that I need to know *now*? I go to blurt it out, but it just seems too big, too important. I don't know where to begin.

"Nothing."

She does look up then. I busy myself finding my calculator.

"Ah, math," she murmurs. "Should I find you a tutor, Owl? Mallory's mother said something about a tutor. . . ."

"I'm fine," I say. "Let's work."

It's late by the time we get to the soup. She got lost in the sketches and I found myself drawn into the winter world she was creating, a world like the one she told me of so many times, when I was a kid and still believed in things like magic.

6

THE WORLD OF WINTER

It was dusk when they came to a new horizon. The land dipped away below them and skeletal trees opened out on to a broad valley, where a dome nestled into the lower reaches of an enormous mountain range. He looked at her, and then the silence was broken by a howl that made ice fall from the branches of the trees. Her ears rang with the shock of it, and she turned, looking for the source of that desolate, yearning sound that warned of danger.

Her companion started beside her, and if there was a spell that had woven them together for their long journey it was broken by that sound. He looked at her, his eyes afraid.

"The wolves of winter. Go!"

He thrust her forward, down the slope to the valley. She scrambled and slipped on soft snow until she was at the bottom, and when she looked back he was standing with his back to her, five wolves before him. They stood shoulder to shoulder, as tall as he, their gray fur rippling in the wind, blue eyes sharp as they looked from her to him.

"What is this?"

"She is my guest."

"She is not fay. We do not like it. She will bring danger."

"She is not a danger. Let me have one day—I have never had company here. Let me know this, and then she will return to her own place."

The wolves stood silent, and she could see even in their stillness the power that had been built into those muscles. She could imagine the hunt. The silent, terrible determination, the speed, the stealth.

"At our howl she must be gone. We give you one day. And be mindful. It is not of the natural order of things. Danger comes of this—you will pay for it one day."

He spread his arms as if helpless and they lowered their heads. And she marveled at him. The power in his own limbs, the way he held his head. His own stillness and silence matched theirs. He was no man she had ever seen the like of before.

7

It's dark when I wake and Mom doesn't believe too much in heating so the apartment is freezing. I put thick socks and a hat on before I even get out of bed, wrapping myself in my quilt and stumbling over to the window.

It was a night of dreams. Of wolves howling and blue fingers that drew frost on windows. Of snow-covered mountains and Avery's strange copper eyes. And now, when I look out of the window, it's like the world was with me. There are no wolves, thank goodness, but on every surface in the darkened street, every rooftop, fence post, and tree, is a fine layer of frost. The cars sparkle clean and white beneath a pearly sky, and only a single set of footprints marks the glittering pavements, still scattered with autumn leaves now curled and frozen. It's all so quiet and so beautiful. Somehow, I guess through Mom's stories, winter has always held magic for me. All the dirt and grime hidden beneath layers of ice and snow. Anything seems possible.

My stomach rumbles. Oatmeal. That's what I need.

I drag the quilt with me into the kitchen. The kettle's on and Mom's looking out the window herself, a faraway expression on her face.

"It's settled properly today," she says. "Yesterday was the first, but this morning is glorious, isn't it?"

"Glorious," I say, shuffling to the cupboard and pulling out the oats. A few spill on the floor. "But I do wish we had a microwave. Or heating."

"The heating *is* on, and here, I'll do the oatmeal." She takes the oats from me. "You make the tea. Could you not find a sweater? The quilt is a little cumbersome, no?"

"It's fine," I say, tucking it around myself and shuffling to get mugs and milk. "Cozy."

"You know it's mostly in the mind," she says. "You start to shiver and your body tenses and then, even if you're not actually cold, your mind thinks you are."

"I am actually bodily cold," I say, pouring boiling water over the tea bags, wondering what would happen if Mom ever saw my hands covered in frost. Was it real? Could it happen again, just like that?

"Goodness, Owl, you're going to scald yourself,"

Mom frets, coming over as I struggle to hold up the quilt while stirring the tea and fretting silently. "Give me that." She whisks the quilt away.

"Hey!" I jump, dropping the spoon. Mum slings the quilt over a kitchen chair and turns back to the oatmeal, and I think she's saying something, but I can't hear her because my skin is screaming at me, tightening as a pale, glittering something sweeps up from my fingertips to my shoulders. I can feel it, curling around the back of my neck and spreading over my scalp, like steel tendons wrapping around me. I look from myself to Mom, not breathing, not moving an inch. It's happening. Right now. Almost as if I predicted it. What do I do? Call out to her? Run? Stand here like a statue until it passes? *Will* it pass? *What is this?*

The room darkens around me and it feels like time has stopped, like I'm stuck in some kind of different world where everything is magnified. I notice cracks in the floor tiles that I've never seen before, the pencil marks up the wall where we've measured my height over the years. The oatmeal bubbles and sputters, an avalanche of sound that threatens to choke me, and Mom's just standing there, in our normal kitchen in our normal world, gesturing with the spoon as she keeps on talking, but if she turned . . . if she turned, what would she see? Would she scream? I imagine the spoon falling from her hand, the oatmeal boiling over, her eyes widening with shock and fear. And there'd be no going back. Nothing would ever be normal again if she saw this. I look down at myself again, hoping that I imagined it, caught up in the bloom of new winter. But as I watch, little flower-like crystals start to spread over my forearms.

They're beautiful.

They're madness.

I snatch the quilt from the chair, fling it over myself, and scamper to the bedroom, shutting the door and leaning against it, my breath bursting out with a hot sob.

I lower the quilt slowly, taking deep breaths, looking down at myself with dread. But my skin is normal again. Normal and cold, with goose bumps. I sit on the bed.

What was that?

It looked like frost. Was it frost? How can it have been frost, on my skin, just like that? Surely such a thing just doesn't exist. Has anyone, ever, in the history of the world, been able to freeze themselves? I've never heard of it. It's impossible.

"It's like something from one of Mom's stories," I tell the owl on the bedpost. It's not a good thought.

"Stupid," I say out loud.

The owl stares at me balefully with its round wooden eyes and offers no reassurance.

"Owl? Are you coming?" Mom calls.

"Yes," I call back, grabbing my heaviest sweater.

"I imagined it," I say to the owl. "That sort of thing just doesn't happen. Does it?"

The owl blinks with a little dry snapping sound.

I flinch away, my breath catching in my throat, and then slowly, skin creeping, lean in toward it.

"Did you blink?" I whisper.

It doesn't answer. Obviously. I stare at it for a little longer, until my eyes ache and my head starts to spin. Then I let myself breathe again. It doesn't move, doesn't do anything. It's a wooden owl, for goodness sake! Mom calls again and I make my way back to the kitchen. I won't think about it. I won't think about anything.

And if Mom notices anything's wrong, I'll demand some proper answers about my father. That will throw her off.

After oatmeal, and thankful that Mom is still a bit wrapped up in her new project, I spend five minutes on Google, keeping half an eye on the completely ordinary non-moving wooden owl. I feel like I've lived about a thousand years already this morning and the day has only just begun. Frozen skin, blinking owls—what next?

Person getting frost on skin: nothing but stuff about frostbite, with some really gross pictures of feet.

Frozen person: all about cryogenic science, freezing

people to bring them back to life.

Frost on skin: some weird beauty treatments and something about uremic frost which is connected to quite bad kidney disease. So then I look up kidney disease, and I don't have that: I'd be really sick and there would be other symptoms.

I feel fine.

And the frost isn't even there now. If that was even what it was. Which it wasn't, because things like that don't happen to human beings.

By the time I get to school I am in no mood to deal with anything else. I just about manage to keep it together for the morning, with Mallory shooting me concerned looks and Avery's strange presence needling me. I keep my head in my books, do the best listening I have ever done in all my classes, and then manage to sit at a table with Conor at lunchtime so there's no chance for private conversation. He's too busy trying to steal potato chips from Mallory and moaning about Avery, who thankfully is nowhere to be seen.

"The guy's a real freak," he says, as if Mallory and I had asked. "Won't talk to anyone, just wanders around on his own, all weird and intense. He's probably been transferred for doing something terrible."

"Like what?" someone asks.

"I don't know," says Conor, flicking his hair out of his eyes. "Like eating the dissection toads or something."

Eeyuch. I tune out and concentrate on trying to stomach my tuna sandwich. Suddenly it tastes toady and disgusting.

"Owl," Mallory says finally, catching up with me as we head toward geography. "What *is* going on with you?"

"I'm fine," I say with a smile.

"You are so not. What is it? Did you ask your mom about your dad? Did she tell you?"

"No, and no."

She corners me, pushing me up against the lockers while people swell around us, her small face determined. She is small, Mallory. A head shorter than me, brown hair pulled neatly back from her face. Her clothes always pristine, unlike mine.

"Mallory!"

"I'm worried. You're not being yourself."

I feel the confusion of everything build behind my eyes while she watches me, concern growing on her face. But it's not like a normal problem, is it, where you tell your best friend and then she says something that somehow makes sense and fixes it? It's not a crush or a fight with your mom. What could she say? What could she do?

"Owl, please . . ."

"You'd think I was crazy. And it isn't even anything anyway."

She shrugs. "So tell me about the nothing. Be crazy. That's fine. At least I'll know about it."

"Not here," I say, as someone bumps into us and I notice Avery heading toward the classroom. "After school?"

"Fine. And you'll tell me everything?"

I nod.

"And in the meantime stop worrying. Whatever it is, it'll be okay."

I do love Mallory. I'm not sure she can fix this, but I know she'll try.

8

"So basically what you're saying is that you have some sort of magical frost power."

"It's not magic!" I yelp, folding my arms. "It doesn't actually *do* anything . . . and I probably imagined it anyway." I shouldn't have said anything. Talking about it with her makes it feel more real.

"But you don't really think that, do you? You wouldn't be worrying about it so much if you did. Why don't you give it a try? See if you can show me?" She's trying to be kind, but I can tell she's having trouble with the idea. Mallory has quite expressive eyebrows and they're doing a lot of expressing right now.

We've just got to the street by her house and there's nobody else around, so it might be worth a try, but I don't actually know how it happens. It's like a sneeze, or a personal sort of storm. It just creeps up on me. I try to explain that to Mallory, but she's determined.

"So, the first time was when I teased you about Avery, and the second time was when your mom took your quilt away. . . . I don't know, is it something about surprise or body heat? Like, if I snatch your hat off right now . . ." She whips it away and throws it over her shoulder, standing back and watching, her eyes bright. "No?" she asks after a minute, when nothing has happened.

"No."

She picks up the hat and hands it back.

"Well, whatever's going on, it obviously doesn't feel like playing right now."

"You don't think I'm making it up?" I breathe out slowly, my chest aching from holding it in. I've been really worried about it ever since I promised I'd tell her. I didn't know how I'd say it all, or how she'd react, and then there was this awful fear that maybe it would manifest and freak her out, or do something terrible like turn her into an icicle.

"No," she says finally. "I just think there must be some logical explanation we haven't worked out yet. Does it hurt when it happens?"

"Not really. Just feels weird."

"And you're not going around hurting anyone else, so there's no big emergency. We'll work it out." She looks at me a little dubiously, then her eyes brighten. "Maybe it has something to do with your dad!"

"Like what, he's a snowman?"

I mean to laugh when I say it, but it doesn't really come out that way, because I'm not finding it that funny. Visions of creatures hiding in the shadows, ice on my skin, it all feels so real, and yet how *can* it be, really?

"It'll be all right," Mallory says as we start walking again. "It's probably just because it's got so cold, and you're tired and worried about things. Maybe it's some kind of static, or a weird skin condition you've inherited, or stress making you shiver. But you should get a *proper* answer from your mom about your dad, even if he's not a snowman. I mean, what's the worst that could happen?"

"I'll try," I say, mostly just to satisfy her. Movement flashes in the corner of my eye, and I turn sharply toward the horse chestnuts that lean their long limbs over the wall from the graveyard. I half expect to see that awful gray creature nestled there, staring at me, but it's just leaves drifting from the gray branches into the alley. I plaster a smile on my face as I turn back to Mallory, hoping she hasn't noticed. "Speak later?"

She grimaces. "Family evening. Probably won't get the chance. But I'll see you in the morning. If we both survive till then!"

I watch her go, feeling a bit envious.

I know it's mean. She really does hate these family evenings. But right now, the idea of being bought pizza and ice cream and sitting with both parents in your normal house, with your normal skin on, while they ask you about your day, sounds pretty good.

9

Normally, when I'm feeling down, I listen to some music, do a bit of drawing, or talk to Mallory. But tonight none of that's working. I avoided Mom when I got in, just called hello upstairs and came into my room. The idea was to do some sketching and lose myself in that, but I'm too agitated, can't settle. The owls I'm drawing are all lopsided and weird-looking, and honestly I'm a bit fed up with owls right now. Mallory's having her "family evening" so she's unavailable. It's probably lucky, actually, since all I'd do is moan and then feel bad about moaning.

"Owl!" Mom's voice interrupts my thoughts. "Come, my love, I've made us some lovely daal."

Daal is lentils.

I cannot tell you how much I loathe lentils.

Mom dresses them up in all sorts of guises: lentil lasagna, lentil stew, lentils in muffins (they're a special kind of horror), and of course the daal. It doesn't matter how many times I tell her that I don't like them, she just keeps on making things with them in her own special way. It's as if she thinks one day I'll turn around and say, "You know what, Mom, I was wrong all along. Aren't these lentils incredible?"

I am never. Going. To say that.

I push my chair back from my desk and storm to the kitchen.

We have a small apartment. My room, Mom's room, sitting room, kitchen. Bathroom. The studio in the attic. Anyway, it doesn't take me long to get to the kitchen. She's dishing up the daal. It's dark out now, and she's lit tea lights all along the kitchen counters and on the table.

"Why don't we have family evenings and order pizza and ice cream and talk about how my day was at school?"

Mom turns to me. She's wearing small gold hoop earrings and they glint as she moves.

"Family evenings?"

"Yes! Special ones, where you make an effort to find out what's going on with me."

"But I already know what's going on with you, Owl—*every* evening is a family evening!"

"Family is all the parts, not just some of the parts."

I'm too cross. It's not coming out right. I take a deep breath, leaning against the wall as she puts the plates on the table. She's made naan bread and raita to go with the lentils, and my stomach rumbles treacherously.

"Family is this." She gestures around the room. "Family is wherever there is home, and food, and love. . . . Come, now. Come and eat, and we'll talk."

"But it's not—"

"Here," she says, reaching into the fridge. "I got your favorite."

Mexicana spicy cheese. She smiles hopefully and my eyes sting.

"I don't want cheese."

"But you love it!"

"I don't want any of this. I want to know who my father is." I fold my arms, glare at her.

"Owl!"

"I need to know!"

She puts her back up against the kitchen counter.

"I've told you the story. I used to read it to you, don't you remember? I told you how I met him, how beautiful—"

"His name, Mom! Tell me his actual real proper name!"

All the color seems to drain from her face as she stares at me and realizes I'm not about to give in this time. My breath catches in my throat and suddenly I feel sick. I wish I hadn't stormed in here, I should have let it go. I'm not going to like it. I can tell from the way she twists her hands that she's scared.

"Just do it," I whisper. How can it be that bad?

"Jack," she says, looking me in the eye. "His name is Jack."

"Jack what?"

"Jack Frost."

Laughing.

Crying.

She's rushing over to me.

I fight her off.

Can't breathe.

Is my life such a joke to her?

Is she crazy, does she really believe what she's saying?

Her eyes are shining with the truth of it.

But how?

How can that be true?

10

THE WORLD OF WINTER

It was a day. It could have been a week, or a month, or longer. It could have been a lifetime. The days in that place did not work the same, and she was lost in the magic that surrounded her so that if it had been forever she would never have questioned it.

The light was low and bright, when it broke through the haze. The mountains towered above them and there were living creatures there: goats tripping over the rocks, and eagles high overhead. A frozen lake opened out to the west of the dome and she was sure it had never been anything other than ice upon ice.

The dome was his palace. Wrought of ice that fractured and splintered light upon shining blue-white floors, there were staircases that led nowhere, and others that swept up to new chambers. Over all was the frozen ceiling, covered in a layer of snow, and where he lit candles the light glanced off a million chiseled surfaces, making fractal shapes upon the floor.

There was danger all around them in that place and she knew when she looked into his silver eyes that he could be just as terrible as any of the wolves, and just as treacherous as the ice.

"What are you?" he asked her. "How do you appear here thus?"

11

I'm in my room, my stomach still churning, eyes stinging. I had to get away from Mom because it can't be true. It can't be. It's ridiculous. Impossible. Plain wrong. I'm shouting the words inside my head to drown out the other thoughts, but they filter through anyway. Because she told me, didn't she, over the years, in all those moon-eyed stories of a winter wonderland, wild and beautiful. And I always knew deep down that my father was not going to be your usual sort of person, Mom being who she is. And then there are the things that have happened since the first frost fell two days ago.

It shouldn't be a big surprise.

My father is an icon of winter, a spirit who spreads frost across the world.

No need to overreact, Owl.

"You *knew* it was going to be something freaky," I tell myself, catching sight of my face in the mirror. There's a full moon tonight and my reflection is a warped glimpse of a new me, someone I suddenly barely know. Pale skin, pale hair, golden eyes—it's me, it just all looks so different right now. The edges seem to blur and I could almost imagine the girl in the mirror *is* some sort of fairy-tale creature, proportions all slightly off, somehow, skin glowing with a strange silver sheen.

What am I?

Something pulls at me deep inside, a fear I never knew about before. What if Mom *is* right and Jack Frost—the figure she made so familiar with all her tales—*is* my father, what would that really mean? Tears gather in my eyes and when I blink they fall into my lap, where they gleam in the moonlight.

Three tiny drops of ice.

"Owl, let me in."

"No!" I brush the tears away, relieved when they melt at the touch of my hand.

"Please, let's talk about it. . . ."

Mom opens the door and lingers there, one hand on the knob.

"I thought you were ready," she says softly. "I thought the stories I told you when you were little might have helped . . . that you would somehow understand. Isn't it better to know?"

"No," I say, and I mean to be brave and turn away from her, and not show her my new, uncertain self, but my voice wobbles and I find myself looking at her while more tears fall and I don't mean to let them. I brush them away as soon as I can, but she sees. She sees everything.

"Oh, Owl!"

"I don't know what to do! What is this? Why am I so *different*?"

"It's all right, my love," she breathes, rushing over to sit beside me on the old bedspread she made with my baby clothes. She puts her arms around me. "You are wonderful. You have always been my wonderful, special girl." She pulls away and looks at me, her eyes bright. "If it is more evident now, then it is not a bad thing, Owl," she says fiercely. "You are becoming what you were always meant to be. I have often wondered . . . and now winter has come, and you're at the age where your body is changing—"

"But not like this! Look!" I howl, as the tears of ice keep on falling.

"They're beautiful. . . ."

"Oh, Mom!" I swipe them away angrily, clench my jaw to stop more coming. "You always say that sort of thing but . . . they're not, they're not supposed to be doing that! What am I going to do? How am I going to go to school? What will I tell people?"

"You're upset," she says, "but that won't last forever. And truthfully I don't know what's going to happen, Owl, and I understand—I understand that to be different is difficult, but you will be all right. Have I not always embraced the part of you that is only you?"

"What do you know about being different?" I demand, pulling away. "I mean, really. When did you last cry tears of ice, or half freeze your best friend with a touch? How do you know what it feels like?"

"Owl!"

"You can't make this better."

"I'm not convinced it *should* be better," she says, looking out into the night sky, her dark eyes glittering. "But if you think there's someone who can help you more, perhaps you should seek them out. I suppose you could . . ."

"You mean *him*?"

"I could never find him again," she says, her voice hushed. "But you're different, as you say. You're *part* of that world I told you stories about, Owl. Come, I'll show you where it all began. . . ."

It's an enormous book, covered in black leather, tucked into the bottom corner of the vast bookshelf that dwarfs the rest of the little sitting room. I recognize it immediately as the one Mom read from when I was a kid. The gold writing on the cover says: *fablef and Earth-fpiritf, how to meet them and how to find your way to your own fpirit felf.*

"This . . ." she says, leafing through the dry, yellowed pages, pulling me on to the settee and switching on the overhead lamp. She peers at me over the top of the book, her eyes twinkling. I think she's enjoying this. It's almost like she's been just waiting for it to happen. I scowl at her. "Well," she says, turning back to the book. "This is what took me to him. I was reading through it, thinking of all these places, of what it would be like if they were real . . . I was searching for something, adventure, I suppose. When I read out the incantation— " she shakes her head, a funny little smile on her mouth "—well, I didn't think it would work."

"But it did?"

"Oh, it did," she says. "All the stories I told you, Owl, some of them were my own. That place I found myself, it was real! I woke in the morning, and I didn't know how real it was—until I discovered I was carrying you."

They were her own stories.

Not fables at all.

"And you think *I* should try this?" I ask.

She bites her lip. "Honestly, I don't think you're

ready. I think you need to find yourself before you can seek answers from others. But . . ." She waves off my protest. "But it's up to you. How can I tell you what to do, or what not to do, in this situation? There has never been another like you, Owl. You, more than most, need to find your own way."

"Oh, just give me the book," I say, taking it and hefting it back to my room.

"Be careful, my love," she calls after me. "Please, be careful."

"I will!" I shout, dropping the book on the bed. I'm shaking, almost numb with exhaustion. I close the curtains and climb into bed, pulling the covers up and heaving the book onto my lap.

I want to talk to Mallory. I look at the clock. Eleven. It's still the same evening. The same day. Just a few hours since I saw her, even less since everything changed. She'd know what to say. I fumble for my phone. No texts, no missed calls. And she had her family evening. I put the phone on the bookcase next to the bed. It can wait. Honestly, what would I even say right now?

"Incantationf," I mutter, opening the book and turning to the index at the back. It must be truly ancient—every single *s* is written as an *f*. Some of my favorite stories aren't there, I realize as I flick through the pages. Of course. Because Mom made them up. They were her experiences of when she went to that other place and met him.

My father.

"Let's do this then," I say, shaking my head as I find a poem that looks a bit like some sort of spell. "Ridiculouf book . . ."

12

Mallory isn't telling me something.

I mean, I'm not telling her something either, but whereas I'm trying to be normal while the name Jack Frost rattles about in the back of my head, she's all bug-eyed and quiet, shuffling along to school, making absolutely no effort to appear normal, and she can't possibly have a Jack Frost situation of her own going on.

"Mall!" I say in the end, after the fifth conversation I've opened gets shut in my face. "What's wrong?"

"I don't want to talk about it," she says, shaking her head.

"But wait, look . . ." I pull at her arm. "Maybe I can help?"

"No, you can't."

"Mallory . . ."

"I just. Can't. I want to get through the day without thinking about it all. Can we do that?"

"Of course we can," I say. "Just, you know, whenever you want to talk . . ."

"Yeah, I know," she says, hitching her bag up onto her shoulder as we reach the main gates. "Did you talk to your mom?"

"Uh, sort of," I say.

"And?"

"Just another bunch of nonsense." I sigh, brushing aside lingering thoughts of frozen tears and fathers with ice-tipped hair and failed attempts to find my "fpirit felf" with that silly old book. "So, let's both get through the day, and maybe we could do something this evening?"

Her face shuts down. "Can't."

"O-kaaay," I mutter behind her back as she storms off into school. Man, that is unlike Mallory. What the heck happened last night? I thought my evening was bad. I try to catch up to her, but she's steaming through the crowds of kids and she's got a very neat way of doing it. I have bigger feet or something—I just don't slink through as easily.

She had her family evening, I remember as we get into homeroom. That must be it. Maybe they nagged about homework, maybe they didn't like the B she got in math last week? I look at her sideways. She's all hunched and pale, playing absently with the zip on her pencil case. Something big has happened. Mallory's pretty tough with all the usual stuff. Maybe . . . maybe they want to move?

"Mall," I whisper. "Mall, are you moving?"

"What?" she looks up, panic all over her face.

"You're not moving, are you?"

And right there, in the middle of homeroom, my ever-bubbly, sensible best friend starts to cry.

"Mallory!"

"God, Owl, why can't you just leave it alone?" she whispers, swiping tears from her cheeks and bending down to her bag, pulling a tissue from the great wad of them she's got in there. "I told you, I just wanted to get through—"

"I'm sorry, I was worried!"

"They're doing a trial separation," she says, keeping her head bent as others filter into the classroom. Conor starts to make his way over, a look on his face as though he's about to prank and wind us up and I shake my head, giving him a good strong glare, which is enough to make him frown and mouth things at me instead. I ignore him and pretend I didn't notice Avery coming in at all, though part of me is treacherously aware of him all the same. "All the fighting, they say it's not fair on me, they want to have a break from each other," Mallory continues.

I shuffle closer, put my arm against hers.

"Oh, Mallory . . ."

"He was packing when I left . . . he's going to stay with my uncle for a few weeks." She puts her head in her hands, and I don't know what to say. I just sit there, right up close to her so she knows I'm here, and then Mr. Varley comes in and starts shouting about people walking in late and scruffy, and it's probably the most normal thing about the day so far, so it's actually quite a welcome sound.

13

"What's with your friend today?"

Avery's very tall. He seems to block out all the light when he falls in beside me on the way to geography. He frowns down at me as if he suspects all the wrong in the world is my doing.

"Personal stuff," I say, trying to get around him.

"Hey," he says, cornering me. "Wait a sec . . ."

He reaches out as if to touch my face.

"What are you doing?" I jolt away.

"It's showing," he hisses.

I put my hand up and feel a fine line of frost just along my hairline.

"It's nothing," I say, brushing at my hair as he watches.

"We both know that's not true," he says. I draw farther away from him, but it's as though the world has shrunk around us. The air is heavy with the smell of woodsmoke. Is it him? Why would he smell of woodsmoke? I look him up and down, noticing again the copper glint in his eyes, the tawny hair, and my mind doesn't want to go there, but there's something about him. Something that makes me think of that old book of Mom's and that other world of magic and impossible creatures.

"You can feel it, can't you?" Avery insists. "We're the same. We're from the same place."

This can't be happening. This is my normal day. This is *school*—nothing's more normal than school, and he's ruining it all. I lean against the wall behind me, putting my hands against the smooth plaster, relieved to have something solid at my back, but my heart stutters as he watches me. My skin prickles and ice spreads around my fingers, blooming out across the wall. I can feel it, though I don't turn to see. I don't want to see. There's a look of something like wonder on Avery's face for just an instant, and then he shakes his head and pulls me away from the wall.

"You need to be more careful," he whispers. "Can't you control yourself at all?"

"I don't know what you mean," I say, pulling away from him. "Who *are* you?"

The main doors bang open and a flurry of autumn leaves spirals in on a cool breath, skittering down the corridor toward us. I gape at the unnatural shapes they're making and Avery takes a deep breath, as if he's about to say something, but before either of us can speak the bell rings, and he strides away from me into the classroom.

Ice on the walls and autumn leaves with a life of their own.

So much for my normal day.

Nothing makes sense. I don't know who Avery is, or where he's come from. How does he know what I can do when nobody else sees it? Geography is torture, and then it's art, and the owl I've been sculpting out of clay is suddenly cringe worthy. There's something so naive about the way it stands there happily on its little branch, as though it's never caught even a sniff of danger. I swear Avery rolls his eyes when he sees it.

How is he in all my classes, anyway? Not even Mallory is in all of them, and we deliberately tried to be.

"Thank goodness that's over," she says when we meet at the gate later, pulling her coat tight against the bitter cold. The sky is a relentless steel gray and the trees are starting to look stark without their leaves. "Nightmare day. Even Conor tried to be nice, and that was probably the worst of all of it."

"He'll have forgotten by tomorrow," I tell her as we

start toward home. "You did it, Mallory. You got through the day."

We got through the day.

"Now I just need to get through the night," she sighs. "What's it going to be like, Owl?"

"I don't know. Weird, I suppose. You could stay at mine. . . ."

"Can't leave her on her own, can I?" she says, scuffing her feet along the ground, her eyes fixed on the pavement. "Thanks though. Maybe at the weekend?"

"Definitely. And you know, she's got friends, hasn't she? She'll be okay, Mall."

"It's just going to be so strange without Dad there," she says. "I mean, he's always there. He's not even one of those dads who goes away to work sometimes. He's just always there, being annoying. . . ." Her voice trails off and I don't know what to say. It's funny, how different our home lives have always been. I suppose everyone's home lives are different. At least I never had any of the fighting. Never really had to worry about Mom, either. She's always been so, well, Mom.

"Maybe it'll be good for them," I try. "Maybe they'll realize how much they miss each other, and he'll come back and they'll be happier."

"D'you think?" She looks up at me with all this hope in her tear-filled eyes, and I feel mean, because it's not likely, is it? And now she'll feel even worse if it doesn't happen.

"Well, it's a *trial* separation," I say, to convince us both. "I mean, that's just the same as taking a break from someone. The point is to miss them and realize how good you've got it, isn't it?"

"I suppose so," she says. "I didn't really think of it like that. It seemed more like they were doing it to get rid of each other."

"Well, we can hope," I say firmly, because there doesn't seem anything else to say. I pull my hat down farther over my head, shivering and hoping I'm not about to start turning blue all over.

"Conor said he saw you talking to Avery earlier," Mallory says with a sidelong look and a bit of a smirk.

"Oh, yeah. That was weird."

"What were you talking about?"

"He asked why you were upset, and I told him 'personal reasons.' Then he just sort of stared at me really . . ."

"He's really got a thing for you!" she says.

"O-o-oh, I don't know," I stammer.

"Ha, you're blushing! It's like love at first sight, Owl!"

"No, it isn't. You don't believe in things like that, anyway."

"Yeah, but you're a bit more receptive, aren't you? And anyway, he's not that bad. Just keeps to himself, from what I can see. And he's quite . . . dramatic looking."

"How about Justin?" I ask, to change the subject.

"Dunno," she says, suddenly all moody again. "He's all with the looks, but, you know, he's still with Daisy. Not right, is it?"

"There's always Conor, you know. . . ."

"Owl!"

"Well, it's true!"

She makes a vomiting sound and we both grin, and then we're on the corner of her street and all the laughter goes out of her eyes.

"I'll text you later," I say, giving her a quick hug. "Hope it's all right tonight, Mall."

"I'll get through it," she says, blowing her cheeks out with a big sigh. "See you tomorrow."

She trails away from me, her footsteps getting slower and slower as she draws closer to her house. It's a nice house—one of those old ones with big bay windows. Her mom works from home, translating legal documents from German to English. There's usually baking going on and amazing cakes, and cookies, to raid from the tin. I wonder if she'll have done any baking today. I imagine walking into the house to find it just a bit quieter and colder, everything the same as yesterday except not, not at all.

I like her mom and dad. They're not exactly gushing. They feel a bit uptight compared to my mom, everything neat and tidy and well organized, their smiles a bit distracted while they check out the mud on your shoes. But they're nice enough.

Poor Mallory.

14

I've made a new decision.

I don't know quite where it came from, but something about today has made everything turn in my head. Like if anything can happen, then maybe I should be trying to make the things I want to happen. I think of Avery, stirring up the wind, telling me we have something in common. The frost in my hair, and the rush of autumn leaves—he knows far more than I do about it all. And then I think of Mallory, who has no control over what's going on at home. And honestly, none of it makes sense. My normal day was about as far as you can get from normal. So, I've eaten my leftover daal like a good girl tonight, and Mom's got half an eye on me but most of her mind is with her work, and I've told her I'm going to study for the math test next week when really

I'm doing some research.

Yep. I'm googling Jack Frost.

There's a movie, where he's a boy, a guardian of the world. And then there are loads of images of him as an old man, laying his hands on the outspread leaves of winter trees, drawing icicles out of gutters, sealing windows with a touch.

When does frost actually appear? Is it really all down to one person? How could one person cover the whole of the world? Because it's always winter somewhere, isn't it? I get lost in my research and find out more than I ever thought I'd know about frost. It's water vapor, basically, which condenses as ice on things like grass and rooftops. But none of it helps me to work out why I'm prone to breaking out in my own private weather storm. And it doesn't help me to control it either. It's happened a few times today—nothing too dramatic, just a feeling that creeps up on me and then there it is: beautiful, frosted shapes on the skin between my fingers, along my jawbone.

"Owl, are you still working?"

I click off Google and pull my book toward me.

"Yes."

"Do you want a hot drink?"

"No, thanks."

"I'm going to work for a bit longer." She pokes her

head in, her eyes slightly distracted, as they always are when she's stuck on something. "Don't be too late, love. School tomorrow . . ."

"Okay."

She pauses, looking me up and down. "Everything all right?"

"Yep. Just . . . working . . ."

"Mmm. Well. Go careful."

Is she psychic? It wouldn't surprise me. Either way, she leaves me to it and after a few minutes I have a really stupid idea.

I'm going to find him.

It's crazy. How does a person go about finding a fairy-tale character? I mean, he's not just going to be dancing over the rooftops, is he? *Is* he? I've tried to tell myself it's all nonsense, but Mom doesn't lie. And normal girls don't cry ice, don't stare out of dark windows imagining what it would really be like if they found Jack Frost and he was their father.

So, I have to try. And if it really is all real, then there will be something between us, won't there? Some sort of frost connection that will lead me to him, or him to me? It's worth a try. I can't just sit here forever anyway, wondering, questioning myself and everything I've ever known. My scalp itches with irritation as I fret over it and when I go to scratch, my hair is crisp with frost. That decides it. I pull on a dark sweater and my boots and prowl through the apartment like a burglar, creeping out of the door when I'm sure Mom's back up in the studio.

It's bitterly cold outside and it rained earlier in the evening, so there are puddles in all the gutters. I tread in one by accident as I head across the road, making for the suspension bridge, and when I look down the water is freezing all around my foot. I reach down to touch it, and where my fingers meet the ice, little veins of white appear, spreading across the surface.

Wow!

I look around, afraid someone will be watching, but nobody's about. It's nearly midnight and too cold for anyone to want to be outside. I tread through all the puddles I can find, a thrill rushing through me every time I turn back to see the trail of frozen water I'm leaving behind me. I jump into the next big one, feeling a bit foolish and a bit excited, completely astounded when a cloud of pale ice crystals rises up around me on impact, spinning in the night air before drifting to the ground. It's like being in a snow globe—my very own little world, all of ice—and for a moment I'm so enchanted, I forget about my mission. And then the moon breaks through the clouds, and the world seems to blaze silver around me. And I remember.

Jack.

I run on, every so often looking around to see the traces of winter I've left behind. The moon seems to urge me onward, onward, and my feet fly faster and faster as the world around me sparkles silver with new frost. By the time I get to the bridge, energy is pumping through my body, a hot-cold sensation I've never known before. I lean against the railing looking up at the moon, a grin spreading over my face at the infinite possibilities that suddenly seem spread out before me. If there's magic in the world then this is it, and I'm *part* of it! The feeling thrills through me and then a creaking sound breaks the silence behind me. When I turn, the whole of the railing has been wrapped in a thick layer of ice that cascades to the bridge itself, sparkling in the moonlight and throwing jagged new shapes onto the hard, frost-covered ground. My fingers look almost like they were cast in ice themselves as they grip the railing, as my heart pounds and the ice spreads, farther, farther, until it feels like I could cover the world with it, standing here forever, just watching the magic take over.

This is Jack's power.

This is mine.

"What is this?" demands a voice.

I spin to see who's speaking but nobody's there.

"What are you? What do you do here?"

I look around again, trying to find the source of the voice. It's not a whisper exactly, but it's not quite normal speech either. It sounds more like the hissing of an old steam train than anything else.

"Answer me!"

"I can't, I don't know. . . ."

There's a soft booming sound and the whole bridge seems to vibrate. I look down to the other end, and I can see it: a tide of ice, coming right at me. And not only on the railings, not only a thin frost of it on the ground, but a great swell, a roaring wall of ice blooming over everything, jagged ridges of it forming on either side and a swath through the middle. The lights on the bridge make the whole thing glow and then, finally, I see a shadowy figure stalking toward me, his arms held low and wide, as if conducting.

Oh, help! I step back, but I'm too late. The tide swells and bursts around me, and I don't think, I just leap up, out of its path, landing awkwardly on warped ridges of ice thicker than I've ever seen. I balance myself, my heart tripping in my chest as he gets closer, and I tell myself, *This is what I wanted. It's what I gambled on.*

I stand in his path, my fists clenched at my sides.

It's Jack Frost.

❄ ❄ ❄

He is like nothing I would ever have imagined. Taller, wilder, more powerful than any of Mom's stories warned me. The air around him blurs with a thousand little shards of ice. His dark hair is tipped with frost, his eyebrows thick with it. He is pale-skinned, the angles in his face shadowed by the blue tinge in the hollows of his cheekbones and beneath his eyes.

"Are you Jack Frost?" my small voice rings out, surprising both of us.

"Some call me thus," he says, leaning forward to study me, his gaze fierce. "And you? You have been making your own small winter here. What creature are you? Do you seek to challenge me?" He tilts his head to one side, his movements all slightly too fast, too stilted, a hungry grin sending a shiver down my spine. "You may, if you wish. I like a challenge, and you may be worthy. I could hear your play half a thousand miles away."

I take a step back. This is not a man. This is not a father. This is an elemental creature who thinks I challenge him. There is nothing in his face of kindness or humanity, nothing I can find there to relate to.

He thinks I am a creature like him.

But I'm not.

I'm. Just. Not.

I turn and run, and there's a crack of brittle laughter

behind me and my whole body is ringing with the shock of it all, my mind a fizzing, confused storm of too many images and too many emotions. I run as fast as I can, for as long as I can. And then I collide with something, and everything goes black.

15

THE WORLD OF WINTER

This was his part of the world, he told her, and there had never been another like her there before. For centuries, since the Norsemen first named him, he had been alone there, his only companions the Wolves of Winter and the Owl, who appeared when he had work to do. She would call him back to her world, he said, and there he would lay the first traces of winter, signaling to all nature that it was time to rest.

It was in her world that he would meet with his brothers and sisters, he told her, while they walked in the mountains. The air was cold and sharp and her breath steamed before her but his did not. All the world around them was an extension of him, there was no part of him that did not fit there.

If he was like no man she had ever known, then his

family were wilder, stranger than he by far. They were the powers of the world, names learned in legend and fable. They were all of Mother Earth's devising: the North Wind, which spread the clouds and whipped up the seas, roaring in full storms and at other times with only a whisper, playing among autumn trees and rattling at the windows. The Queen of May, who heralded new beginnings, and Lady Midday, who brought heat wave and summer madness. The autumnal Earl of October and the wise old Green Man, and the Lady of the Lake, who has her own kingdom beneath clear waters. He did not see them often, he told her, only when they were called to Mother Earth's Royal Fay Court by the lesser spirits, the winged fairies and the tiny, nimble sprites, all in tribes dedicated to air or fire, water or earth, that they remember their duty to her and do their work as it should be done.

"Even in chaos there is order," he said. "Every thing leading to another, keeping the world alive. . . . We are part of that cycle."

She did not know if she was awake or if she dreamed. She did not question as he held her hand and led her safely up crumbling, shifting hills of snow, as the light changed, and the blue-white shadows over the land grew longer beneath the pale sun. She listened to his stories and heard his loneliness and her own heart panged for she knew that she was only a brief interlude for him, and he for her.

"It does not change," he said, looking out over the lake. "All is still here, all is quiet. Sometimes it is what I need, when I have been in the world of men and seen the creep of concrete, the swell of smoke on the horizon. And sometimes I am angry when I am here, for it is my prison, and when I am let out it is only to do my duty. I cannot make the world a different place, I can only do just as I should. It is all I am, all I was made for."

"And yet," she said, finding her voice in a cloud of steam. "And yet you have some power and liberty. You have form and feeling, does that not count? Does that not make you capable of something more than your limits?"

He did not answer her, then. His silver eyes gleamed as he looked down at her, and then he swept her up with him, sliding and tumbling down the hill, landing in a spray of snow and ice, and she flailed on that frozen lake but he did not. His bare feet were firm as though they were on solid ground and as the sun set, turning the whole world a rose-gold pink, he showed her how to dance.

16

I open my eyes to darkness so complete that for a moment I think I haven't opened them at all. Then the moon breaks through the clouds and a face appears. Familiar, and not familiar. Probably the last face in the world I need to see while I'm lying all confused on the ground.

Avery.

He reaches down to help me sit.

"Are you all right? What were you doing?" he asks.

"I don't know. . . ." I shift back, straining my eyes until I've worked out that we're beneath a massive oak tree in the middle of a field. It's the old park. I've flown kites here, made daisy chains, tried my best at cartwheels (Mallory put me to shame, every time), shared picnics with Mom, but I'm not sure I've ever been here in full night. All the shapes that would normally be so familiar are like little bits of nightmare: fences creaking, spiny trees clustered together like gnarled old men, and for a moment, I'm sure I see strange shapes darting along the bushes in the distance, little otherworldly creatures, ready to chase and pounce and gibber and howl.

When I look back there's nothing at all, just a solid line of black where the bushes are. I shake my head and pull myself up against the tree, ignoring the wobble in my knees. If there *was* something there, it's gone now.

"What are we doing here?" I ask, making my voice firm. "Why are you here?"

"You rushed into me," he says. "Don't you remember? You came right at me and then sort of collapsed. I staggered about a bit and then managed to carry you here."

"But why?" I look around as a low autumn breeze begins to play with the leaves on the ground, picking them up and shuffling them like cards before throwing them out in all directions. I give Avery a sharp look as my hair blows back from my face. His eyes are focused on the leaves, his expression distracted. "Why you? Why here?"

"I don't know! I was lucky, I suppose." He shakes his head, the leaves drifting silently back to the ground. "I didn't know where else to take you. I don't know where you live! What were *you* doing out there, anyway?"

"I was looking for . . . someone."

He stares at me. "Did you go looking for Jack? Did you find him?"

What did I find? Not what I was looking for. I try to forget the way Jack looked, the way he acted when he saw me.

"How do you know I was looking for Jack?"

"I know who you are," he says, his voice gentle. "I told you, we come from the same place. And even if I didn't know before, it's clear. It shows on you."

"What shows? What place?"

"You're connected to Jack. You have the same way with ice and frost. There were rumors of a daughter . . ."

"Rumors?"

"At the Royal Court," he says. "The Royal Fay Court of Mother Earth."

He says it with such reverence. *The Royal Fay Court of Mother Earth.* All the little bits of nightmare seem to come to life again, and for a moment I think that perhaps I'm just going to drown in all of this, that nothing will ever be the same again, no matter what I want. Then I think of Mom discovering my empty room. How long have I been out? It must be hours by now.

"I have to go," I tell Avery, dragging myself away from the tree. "I can't just sit around here under trees all night. I've got to go home."

"Let me help you," he says as I stagger forward, narrowly avoiding colliding with him.

If everything else weren't quite so overwhelming, I'd be dying of embarrassment just from all this swooning around in front of him. Not that he looks overly bothered by it. In fact I wonder, as I look up and see the way his copper eyes shine, if he's even enjoying it all.

"No, thanks," I say, my voice stiff. "I'll manage."

"Owl . . ."

I look up at him. All I can see in his face is concern, kindness even.

"I'm not going to hurt you. We're not all monsters."

But that's exactly what I think Jack is. And maybe so am I. Maybe the whole world *is* full of monsters and Avery is one of them, no matter how kind he might be acting.

"I need to go."

I turn my back on him and make to stride away, but I don't get very far. My knees are trembling, my head suddenly starts to throb, and for a second I think I'm going to throw up. I pull away when I feel his arm around my waist, but I don't have the energy to do it properly, and actually there's something quite comforting about the way he smells, reminding me of bonfires and roasting chestnuts.

“Where are we going?” he asks in a mild tone.

“Cumberland Road,” I mutter.

And there you have it. Dragged back home by the weirdest, most unknowable boy in school, after an evening spent freezing puddles and being petrified by my supernatural father.

Not a lot of room for normal anymore, I’d say.

17

I wake all in a hurry, thrashing my arms around and jumping up, pulling myself out of a frozen sea as a massive old iron boat comes right at me, darkened hull creaking beneath sheets of ice. The mast is a mass of icicles that could fall at any moment and on the deck are legions of strange, shadowy creatures, all of them watching me with glowing eyes.

"Owl?"

Out of the darkness, my mother's eyes, round and bright. She comes toward me and puts her hands on my arms, pushing me back to sit on the edge of my bed as the familiar shapes of the room come into focus.

"What was that?" she asks.

"Uh. Dreaming."

"Did you try the incantation again?"

"No."

"Where were you, Owl?" Her voice is soft with relief, or worry, I can't tell which. I try to keep my mind on the here and now but memories of last night keep crashing over me, one after the other. Frozen puddles. The bridge beneath the moon. Jack Frost, striding toward me over a sea of ice. The tree. Avery.

"Owl?"

"What time is it?"

"Six."

I groan and fall back onto the bed. "Need more sleep . . ."

"I'll wake you in an hour. And Owl?"

"Mmm?"

"We're going to talk tonight. I'll even buy the pizza and the ice cream."

"Mm. 'Kay."

She lets out a small huff of impatience and leaves me to it.

It's warm in the apartment this morning. I feel like I could lie here forever and let all the busy buzzing thoughts float around just outside of the part of my brain that cares.

And later there'll be pizza and ice cream. A proper family evening. I mean, without my father, of course. Can't imagine him sitting there with cheese all down his chin.

Mallory!

I roll over, grab my phone, and look at it.

Oh, no. Three missed calls and two texts, all from Mallory last night.

Hey, can we talk? Know it's late, been a terrible evening . . .

Where are you?

I said I'd text her and I completely forgot.

So sorry.

I text, my tongue stuck between my teeth as I consider the lie I'm about to tell her. I can't exactly describe all that happened in a text, can I?

Was doing homework, fell asleep. See you in a bit? Sorry it was awful Mall, big hug xxxx

I press Send, a niggle in my belly from lying to my best friend. I'll tell her everything, I decide. As soon as I've made up for not being around last night. I'll get her to believe me, somehow.

The second I see Mallory, standing on the corner of her street, leaning against the wall with her arms folded, I know it's not going to be the day I tell her about my father.

To be honest, it's kind of a relief. I walk up to her knowing that I don't have to even try to explain everything that happened last night: how Jack looked, the power that came from him, how I ran away straight into Avery. I still don't know how I feel about it all. Jack's not the father I dreamed of, that's for sure. He wasn't even like the man I pictured when Mom told her stories. She always said he was wild, I just didn't know what that really looked like until last night.

So, I'm just going to lie through my teeth.

Normal is back on the table.

"Hey, Mall," I say.

"Hey, Owl." She sounds really distant and weary.

"Sorry about last night."

"It's all right," she says with a glance at me as we start walking. "You look terrible. You must be coming down with something."

"Yeah, probably." I sniffle. "But, anyway, do you want to talk about it?"

She doesn't speak for what seems like a really long time, and I'm starting to feel a bit awkward, wondering if

I should ask again or change the subject, when she finally opens up.

"It was just so weird," she says. "The house was really quiet, and Mom was doing all the usual things—you know, making dinner, asking about school, moaning about work—but it all just felt wrong. Then Dad phoned me just after dinner, and she left the room because she knew it was him. And he was all forced-happy about Uncle Simon's spare room smelling of socks, and how he hoped I was going to do my homework . . . and I felt a bit like screaming then, because what does that really matter right now? Anyway, then Mom came in and she didn't ask about him but she was acting all awkward, like she didn't know what to say, so I told her about the socks thing and she made this comment about Uncle Simon always being a bit immature, as though that's what Dad is being like. . . ." She trails off, shaking her head. "And I just felt so angry with them both for messing things up and then not even talking about the right things, y'know? Like it's all business as usual and nobody's got any *feelings* about anything!"

"It sounds really awkward. . . ."

"Yeah. It was." She huffs and tucks her chin into her scarf. "It's *so* cold today!"

"Freezing," I say, though to be honest it hadn't really

occurred to me. Maybe it's a Daughter-of-Jack-Frost thing? I pull my hat on anyway and hunch my shoulders a bit, scuffing my feet along the frozen pavement. After a moment Mallory threads her arm through mine and it feels good. Like she's helping, even if she doesn't know it.

I will tell her. Just not yet.

18

The day seems to be going quite well, despite ever thing that's happened, and I'm just starting to relax about it all and tell myself that I have it under control, and then science happens. I'm so busy congratulating myself on my "normality" that I'm not really concentrating on the experiment and, when I see the contents of everybody else's test tubes have gone a misty brown color, I panic. My fingers instantly turn from white to pale blue, little patterns of frost breaking out over the bench where I'm working. I look desperately to my left, where Gavin and Mark are playing with the Bunsen burner. They haven't noticed anything, but still the frost is spreading, inch by inch, eating up the dark wood in a great, pale, sparkling tide, getting closer to them every second. I take a deep breath, my eyes scanning the room, sure that at any moment someone's going to notice.

Of course, someone does.

Avery meets my panicked stare with a frown and his eyes widen when he sees what's going on. I shrug in desperation as the bench begins to creak beneath the frost. Everyone else is concentrating on their experiments, and Mrs. Launder is busily writing *"Points for discussion"* up on the board in her spidery handwriting.

"What do I do?" I mouth at Avery, my heart thumping in my ears as I clench my hands into fists and try to think of fire, or deserts, or hot coffee, anything that might stop this from becoming a major disaster.

Suddenly all the windows on the other side of the room bang open, a fierce wind howling through the class. Papers fly, test tubes fall and smash on to the benches. Mrs. Launder hurries over, her scarf flapping in the wind, and starts ordering people to help her shut the windows. Gavin and Mark race to make the most of the chaos, their feet crunch on broken glass, and suddenly my corner of the room is empty. Avery strides over, his hair standing up even more wildly than usual, cheeks red with exertion.

"Thank you," I breathe, keeping half an eye on the rest of the class as he peers down at the bench. "I don't know what happened. . . . I just . . ."

"Don't worry about it," he says.

"What do I do with it?"

"It's not thick ice," he replies. "Just a bit of frost. Look . . ." He drags his forearm over the bench and leaves a swath of damp wood behind.

"I don't think it'd do that if I tried."

"Perhaps not," he concedes, his eyes gleaming as he looks at me. "You'd probably just make a gang of mini snowmen. . . ."

"Hey!" I can't help but smile at the image.

"Well, anyway," he continues, brushing at the frost with his hands. "All sorted now." He looks up as Mrs. Launder starts to hand out dustpans and brushes. She gives us a sharp look, instantly ordering us to help in the cleanup, and we trail over, crisis averted. I look at Avery out of the corner of my eye as Mrs. Launder shoves a broom in my direction and he winks at me, a playful look on his face as the leaves skitter around my feet.

"Hey," I whisper. "Stop it. . . ."

"What?" he asks, eyes full of innocence.

"You should work a bit harder on the whole control thing," he says at lunchtime. Somehow we've ended up in the line together, though I was trying to have a break from him and everything else, just for five minutes. He frowns down at the baked potato I've absentmindedly paired with mashed potato.

"I know," I say. "But can't we just forget about it for now, please?"

"I'm not trying to argue with you," he says.

"I don't know what to do about it all," I hiss, shuffling along the line, grabbing some juice and thrusting money at the cashier. "I mean, it's not like you've shared much about what *you* know. . . ."

"You really think you're ready to hear it?" he asks, drawing me to one side.

"Do I have any choice? I can't keep on doing this!"

"Okay," he says, his jaw clenching. "I'll help. Maybe if you know more you'll be able to stop making these mistakes."

"Mistakes?"

He sighs. "You're not in control of the power you have, and it's not like Jack's going to help you. So. Meet me by the tree. Seven o'clock." He gives me a funny, crooked little smile. "We'll figure it out."

"Okay," I manage, trying to smile in return. I feel flushed and sick and I'm not at all sure that I'm making the right decisions. Wouldn't it be better just to pretend that nothing's happening? Would it go away if I just ignored him and left it? Do I really want all this? Is there any choice? My spine tingles as I work myself up and I know then. I have to face it. "I'll be there."

❄ ❄ ❄

"What was all that about?" Mallory asks when I sit down. My hands are shaking so much I nearly drop the tray, and she has to rescue it for me. "Owl, what's going on? Was Avery hassling you? Why do you have all this potato?"

"He's just intense," I say, putting my head in my hands, trying to calm down before I start freezing everything in sight. "And I don't know about the potato. . . . I'm a bit all over the place today."

"I noticed," she says. "You're sure it's not down to him?"

"No, it's just . . . the stuff we talked about before. You know."

"That magic stuff? You don't *really* believe all that, do you?"

The scorn in her voice feels a bit like a slap.

"Just forget about it," I hiss, blinking back tears. "You don't need to be worrying about me anyway. You've got enough of your own stuff going on!"

"Thanks for reminding me," she says, sticking her chin out and reaching for her bag, shaking her head. "Maybe you're right. Maybe we've both got too much going on. I'm not going to force it out of you—if you don't want to tell me stuff that's fine."

I stare at her as she stands in a hurry, chair flying back, cutlery clattering on the tray as she shoves it away. It feels like the whole room has quietened, like everyone's watching. Conor is full of interest across the table, his eyes bright with the drama. I grip the sides of my chair hard with my hands and *will* myself not to start freezing things around me.

"Mallory, wait—"

"I'm going," she says, flushed and bright-eyed. "I just can't do this right now." She walks off, weaving her way through the throng, quickly joined by Conor. I should go after her. I should make it right, tell her everything, but I can't. I'm too confused. I'd just make it worse, and if we got into another argument I don't know what might happen. I need to find out what Avery's got to say, and then maybe I'll know what the heck's going on and what I can possibly say to explain it all.

It's a really awful, lonely walk home. I did linger at the gate for a while, but there was no sign of Mallory, and after a few minutes I got fed up. I mean, what is she even really cross about? That it's hard for me to tell her my father's Jack Frost and I'm some kind of supernatural frost girl? Well, excuse me, Mallory Freidman, I'm not sure you'd be handling it so well, either. I stomp all the way back to the apartment, angry with everything, surrounded by the evidence of my father's power over the world and desperately trying to ignore the creeping feeling that someone or some*thing* is following me, watching me all the way. Every leaf that falls makes me jump. Every shadow seems to be teeming with activity.

It's only my imagination.

Isn't it?

19

THE WORLD OF WINTER

The wolves bayed from the topmost mountain ledge and she knew how they felt. This world was heartbreaking in its beauty and its treachery. From every ledge hung lethal spears of ice—in every footstep was uncertainty. He looked from the wolves to her and raised his hands to her face.

"You have been the brightest dream," he said, his silver eyes looking straight into hers.

"Am I only a dream?"

"There is no other possibility. No mortal I know of may tread here. You are not of the fay. You are a dream."

She raised her own hands and touched his face, from

his brow down to his chin, and he was colder, colder than he had been in the morning when they began. She saw that he was withdrawing from her, that for him, truly, she would never be more than a memory.

"What do we do now?" she asked.

"Now?" He smiled, a wicked glint in his eye. "Now we run!" He took her hand and pulled her along with him, and her feet were clumsy through the feathered snow and over the ice, but his footsteps carried them back, back toward the woodland where they found each other. Vines hung from brittle, age-darkened branches and curling roots sought to trip them, but he did not slow his pace and finally they reached the clearing in the center, where sky met sky and only snow rested between.

"Ah," he said, looking up. "Here she is, my wisdom . . ."

High overhead soared the great owl he had spoken of, her soft voice calling out, echoing through the woodland.

"Time."

"Winter comes," he said, his eyes brightening. "It is time for me to leave."

The Owl stared at the girl with fierce, golden eyes and in them she saw her own future, that this place would stay with her always, even if she was never here again. So she did not fight when he gave her one last look and turned to leave, though she felt colder and more alone than she had ever thought possible. She would have given anything, in that moment, to stay with him. But she drew herself in and watched in silence as he walked away. The Owl flew down in a great scattering of snow to land on his shoulder, and when she opened her eyes the dream was over.

A new reality was begun: one that would stay with her forever.

20

"Owl McBride, do not walk out of that door."

"I need to, Mom!"

"I bought pizza. And ice cream. And now you're off out into the dark, in all this cold . . ."

"The cold doesn't bother me." *Not since I went out to find Jack.* "You should know that."

"Very well," she says, reaching around me and closing the door. "But it bothers me. Call it maternal instinct, if you will. Now where are you going? And where were you last night?"

"I was with Mallory. Her mom and dad are having a trial separation and she's really upset. I just wanted to help."

"Oh, poor Mallory," Mum says, her face softening. "And poor Lily and Edward. Is there anything I can do?"

"No," I say, heat rushing to my cheeks. "I don't think so. I just want to be there for her, you know."

Mom disappears back into the kitchen and comes back a second later holding a shopping bag.

"The ice cream," she says, handing it to me. "We'll still need to have our talk, Owl, but it can wait until tomorrow." She leans in and kisses me on the cheek. "You're a good friend."

"Thanks, Mom," I whisper, past a sudden lump in my throat. I open the door and rush out of there while I can still breathe.

All this lying is choking me.

"You brought ice cream," Avery says, when I drop the bag down by the roots of the ancient tree. He's sitting up against the trunk, looking like he's been here for hours and could comfortably stay for hours longer. He reaches over and takes the tub. "But there are no spoons. . . ."

For goodness sake.

"Mom thinks I'm visiting Mallory," I say, sitting down, glad he was here waiting for me. I'm still getting that unsettling feeling of being spied on. When I look around, inevitably there's nothing there, but it's beginning to wear. "So, no spoons."

He starts digging around in his pockets. He's kind of

long and lean, and he always wears dark colors. Tonight he's got cargo pants on and a black hoodie: plenty of pockets to search through.

"What are you looking for?" I ask eventually.

"Here," he says, pulling out a small knife with a wooden handle. "Do you think this will do?"

"For what?" I ask, shuffling back, a chill spreading over my scalp.

"Don't be stupid," he says. "For the ice cream, obviously."

"Well, I'm not going to be using it," I say.

"You don't want any?" He looks up, genuine surprise on his face.

"No!"

"You don't mind if I . . ."

"Go for it," I say, shaking my head as he snaps open the lid. Man, does he like ice cream. That, or he hasn't eaten yet today. He wolfs down about half of it without looking up. It's making my teeth ache just to watch him.

"So, about everything," I start eventually, getting a bit bored of waiting while he stuffs his face. "You were going to tell me. . . ."

He stiffens, and stabs the knife into the remaining ice cream, putting it down hard on the ground.

"You're sure you want to know?" he asks. "Your eyes look a bit wild already."

"I keep getting this feeling." I shrug. "It's probably nothing."

"What feeling?"

"Like someone's spying on me."

He frowns. "When? Where?"

"I don't know. Through the window at home, on my way home from school." I try to brush it off. "I'm probably just feeling spooked about everything else. I haven't actually *seen* anything. Would there be something? Are there creatures like that, who follow people and spy on them?"

"There are all sorts of creatures out there," he says, his eyes roaming the dark field. "I don't know why they'd be stalking you, though. You're probably right about being spooked. I guess it's a lot to take in, if it's all new to you. . . ." He turns to me. "You really didn't know anything till now?"

"Nothing," I say, my voice tight. "A week ago everything was just normal. Mom used to tell me these fairy tales, but I thought that was all they were. Stories. I had no idea . . ." There's a little tug in my chest when I think of how simple things seemed then. When the only mystery was over the identity of my father, and it could have gone so many different ways. "Anyway. What about you? How long have you known you were different?"

"Always," he says. "I grew up with the fay, mostly.

I've never really known anything else. So—" he stands—"here's the deal. If I tell you stuff—about me, and the rest of it—you have to swear you'll never say where you heard it."

"Okay, I swear."

"Properly, I mean. Put your hand on the bark—" he reaches up and puts his hand against the tree "—here, and swear on Mother Earth that you will never tell anyone where you learned of what I'm about to tell you."

"Really?"

"Really," he says. "This isn't playtime, Owl. The stuff you want to know is serious."

"I swear on Mother Earth that I will never tell anyone where I learned of what you're about to tell me," I say, putting my hand on the rough trunk of the old tree as a sudden wind rushes over the field, blowing my hair up around my face and making the branches of the tree shudder.

"Good," says Avery. "Let's walk."

"Walk?"

"I'm not made of frost," he says with a grin, "even if you are. The ground is already freezing here."

I scramble up and he hands me the ice cream tub, taking the knife out and licking it clean before putting it in his pocket.

"You're sure you're done?" I ask.

"Yes, thank you," he says, looking up at the sky. "We'd better be quick. There was talk of snow today and Jack will be about at some point. I don't really fancy bumping into him right now."

"Is he that bad?" I remember that hungry grin, the inhuman way he moved, and shudder at the memory, quickly looking over my shoulder as if he might be there. Nothing. Nothing but darkness and shadows, and the golden glow of the streetlights.

"Not *bad*," Avery says. "Just very . . . Jack."

"What does that mean, though?"

"He's an elemental, and one of the stronger ones. There's him, the North Wind, the Lady of the Lake, and a couple of others we don't have so much to do with here. They're not like humans, not like anything else at all, really."

"And you grew up with all of them?"

"Since I was small," he says, avoiding my eye as we head toward the river.

"What's it like?"

"They're big characters—kind, cruel, wild, nurturing, all the things you'd expect from nature, I guess." He grimaces, as if it's an effort to talk about it. "It's not a bad place to grow up. You're never alone, never without some kind of mischief going on. . . ."

"And Mother Earth is in charge of it all? What's she like?"

"I've never *met* her!" he says incredulously. "She's *Mother Earth*!"

I blink at him, feeling out of my depth. What do I know about anything? If I hadn't lived through the last few days I'd be laughing in his face about now.

Avery sighs with exaggerated patience. "She's the leader of the fay, and of all the natural world," he says. "She's the head of the Royal Court, of course, but nobody's seen her for a long time. I mean, she's not exactly one of the fay—she doesn't involve herself in all the everyday stuff."

"Okay." I nod. "So what does the Royal Court do then?"

"Keeps an eye on things generally." He shrugs. "The leaders meet in the Old Druid Wood every few months to make decisions on her behalf. It's an ancient fay site."

"Is Jack fay? Does that make me half fay?"

"Yes," he says, looking me up and down as if wondering if I really measure up to that.

"What kind of fay creature are you?" I ask. It sounds awful as soon as it leaves my mouth. Avery shakes his head with a smile. "Sorry," I add, "but I mean, if I'm Jack Frost's daughter, then that makes some sense, because of all the frost. But you have the thing with the wind and all the leaves—what's that?"

"Autumn," he says. "My father is connected with

autumn. He's part of the Royal Court, but he's not as powerful as yours." His eyes darken as he speaks and he picks up his pace.

"And how do you . . . I mean, how do you control what you do?"

"There are risks." He shrugs. "Being half human isn't exactly normal there. I always knew I had to be careful not to get lost in the magic of it all. I've got to look after my human side, too. . . ." He gives me a sidelong glance. "Guess we both do."

"But if you're half human . . ."

"Only physically," he says. "Anyway. Enough about me. What about you? What's it like growing up normal? What's your Mom—"

But I don't get to hear what he was going to ask, because as we get to the river, a roaring wind seems to pick up out of nowhere, pushing our hair and clothes back, making me stagger. Avery grabs my hand and pulls me into the old tunnel beneath the bridge, swearing.

"That was the wrong way to come," he says, his eyes darting out into the black of night.

"Is it Jack?" I try to peer around him, but he shoves me back into the damp stone wall.

"No. It's the North Wind."

"Is that so bad?"

"If he were to see us together—that could be bad."

A piercing, shrieking gust barrels visibly down the tunnel, rippling the air. Avery pushes back against me, as if to hide me completely, as the enormous figure of an old man with a long beard appears at the end of the tunnel, starting toward us.

I struggle against Avery, partly out of pride and then because it's hard to breathe against his back, and then there's another commotion: the sound of cannons firing, or of rocks being thrown into the water. It takes me far longer than I'd like to extricate myself, and by the time I manage to break free, the old man is nowhere to be seen.

"What's going on?" I demand.

"Jack called him out," Avery whispers, his hand still on my arm, stopping me going forward. "We've got the two of them out there, now. This is a nightmare!"

"Why?" I hiss, pulling away from him. "What's wrong with you? I thought this was your kind of thing!"

More booming, more howling.

"What are they doing out there?" I ask curiously.

"Playing," Avery says in a disgusted tone, sliding down the wall of the tunnel to sit on the ground. "You go and join them if you like. I'm staying here."

I suppose I should be a mess by now. I mean, Jack Frost, the North Wind? Boys who make you swear on ancient trees? Skin that frosts over when you're stressed? I wouldn't have believed any of it a week ago, but now it's here, right in front of me, and I recognize that the knock of my heart in my chest isn't plain fear. I mean, it's a little bit of fear, sure, but it's also a massive dose of energy and excitement, because I'm looking out from the tunnel to the sort of sight I thought I'd only ever see in movies or in my own imagination. And it's wild and scary and beautiful and so elemental and powerful, it's as though all the world was gray and flat until right now.

Jack Frost is having a snow fight with the North Wind.

I'm guessing normal people just don't see this stuff. They see the snow being hurled by the wind, they see ice forming off the ridges of the bridge, and then they lower their heads and fight their way through, never seeing the figures who caper and charge at each other.

"You're actually buzzing off this, aren't you?" asks Avery, appearing at my elbow, his voice incredulous.

"It's amazing!"

"You're not afraid?"

"Well, they haven't seen us. They're having too much fun to bother looking."

He gives me a funny look.

"I don't get it," I say. "Why are you so worried about it?"

"They're dangerous!" he says. "These are enormous,

powerful beings, capable of mass destruction, and they're just playing out there! They have serious business, and this is what they spend their time doing. Anything could happen!"

"You're scared!" I say, turning to him properly while the elements rage happily outside.

He flinches away, as if I slapped him. "I am not scared," he hisses. "You're just being naive. You've no idea about the real world, nobody has."

"So I'm trying to learn! I want this, Avery! I want to know more. I want to know *him,* even if it does scare me! If you don't like it, you should just go back home and leave me here."

"I can't just leave you!"

"You can," I say, taking a deep breath and trying to reassure him. "I'll be fine. I need to do this. You don't."

He gives me a long, level look. "Fine," he says eventually, putting his hood up and digging his hands into his pockets. "But be careful. It might not be what you expect."

He turns and walks down to the other end of the tunnel, and then he hesitates for a moment, as if unsure whether to leave me here or not.

"I'm fine," I whisper. "Just go." A thin cloud of vapor comes out of my mouth as I speak, crystallizing in the air and zipping off toward Avery. It spatters against his back and he turns, shaking his head, before sloping off into the distance.

Whoops! That's not going to make me popular.

Not that I'm very popular with anyone right now.

Maybe I'll skip school on Monday.

I turn back to watch the two wintry figures as they start skating on the frozen river. It makes me smile. Avery's right. They're two powerful, elemental figures who look like they'd be all about ruling the world and dominating mankind, and there they are, playing! I venture out of the tunnel as they rush out of sight and stand there in the blizzarding snow, lifting my head to the sky as the wind buffets me.

"Aha!" booms a voice, as the thundering sounds of winter come closer once more. "There she is: the little pretender!"

Part Two

21

FABLES & EARTH SPIRITS

The North Wind

The ground shook as he strode toward her and when he spoke, the world vibrated with his words. Her stomach turned, and her hair streamed back from her face as he came closer, and she could not understand what he said, for he spoke in the language of thunder and all she could hear was the shudder of his power.

He rose up above her, twice the size of a mortal man, and she lowered her head and gripped herself tight and tried to steal breath from the wind that tore at her. Beneath her feet was a tide of sand that stung her skin and rose up to burn her eyes, and all around them was a howling, desolate void that blocked out the sky itself. In that instant she wished with all her heart that she had not uttered the words that got her there, but the heart does not make much of bargains and has no power at all over the elements.

"I cannot change it for you."

The girl lifted her head, for they were the first words she had truly understood. His blue eyes bore into hers and there was sympathy there, but she saw that it would change nothing.

"You struggle here and if I could, I would make it less," he said, his long white beard dancing with a thousand eddies. "But I am what I am and this is my world, child, it is made of all that I am, and all that I am is this. . . ."

He winked and spread his arms wide, and the wind roared. Tiny figures seemed to ride the storm, whooping and twisting as it tossed them around, their wings like shards of silver. He smiled at their antics, but when she tried to look closer they vanished, and the girl wondered if she had imagined them entirely. She thought to ask him, but her voice was lost as he stooped low, until his face was mere inches from hers. He was ancient, and yet the years did not show upon his skin, only in his eyes. She marveled at him even as she knew she should be afraid. There was nothing he could not do here, no battle she could win, should he choose to fight.

"Go home, child," he rumbled. "This is not your playground, you are not fay—it is not safe for thee here, and I would not see thee hurt."

22

When you don't have a father you can make up your own version. He's not going to read you a story, or make fiery chilies that nobody can actually eat, but if he were there, those are the things he'd do. And he'd be tall and broad and a bit messy, a bit absent-minded, and he'd get cross if you messed with his books, but he'd give you great hugs when you needed them, and he'd always be there when you needed help with homework or had an argument with your mom.

I've made up various versions of my father over the years. None of them were like the figure who stands before me now. Pale as ice and sharp-featured, he stands there as if he owns the world and never has a doubt in his mind. Everything seems to blur around him as he moves in his strange, staccato way, his shadow long and lean behind him in the moonlight. He's wearing layers of gray clothes, most of them covered in snow, and every time he exhales it lets out a little cloud of ice particles. The figure of his friend is in the distance now, blowing a blizzard around a couple who are rushing along the river path, clinging to each other, heads lowered against the snow.

"Is that really the North Wind?" I ask.

"Who else would it be?" Jack Frost replies, looking back. He turns back to me and frowns. "Speaking of names, which have you?"

Can I really tell this creature who I am? Do I want him to know?

"My name's Owl," I manage, through the roaring in my ears.

"Owl!" His eyes narrow. "Favored by Mother Earth . . . But what are you? You have something of a human aspect about you."

"I am human! *Half* human, anyway."

"Half human . . ." He narrows his eyes, tilting his head. "And what of the other half, Owl?"

"Do you remember a woman?" I ask, my voice trembling. "Thirteen years or so ago: dark hair, brown eyes, a bit crazy?"

He steps back, his face darkening.

"I'm half fay . . . half whatever *you* are," I whisper, looking up at him, close enough to touch, feeling the cold emanate from him and remembering all the times I *wanted* him to be there, all the sports games and the school plays and the birthdays when his absence was like a physical presence, like a shadow by my mom's side. All the times I wondered why he wasn't there.

I mean, not that I wanted Jack Frost to wander in, late and dripping ice, having to stand at the back with Mom because all the seats were full of more organized parents.

"You're my father."

"That . . ." he says, looking me up and down, his eyes haunted. "That is not possible, Owl-creature. I am an element of nature. Things like family, fatherhood, they're not a part of my existence. They are of the human domain. However . . ." His face brightens. "You certainly have something of the winter about you. Shall we see?"

"See what?"

"Come," he calls, racing out onto the icy river. "Come and show me what you have, my little pretender!"

I'm standing on the riverbank, watching Jack's bare feet dance across the ice as though it were a ballroom floor, patterns curling out around him, and I don't know whether the world is shrinking or growing, but there's an exploding sort of feeling in my chest because nothing is ever going to be the same after today. He shut me down so quickly, rejected me so easily, I can't help but feel tight and small about it. And yet, watching him out there, so unhindered, spinning in a hailstorm of his own creation, how can I expect anything different? I'm stuck. I can't move toward him, and I can't move away. I just stand there, watching him, while a lifetime of hope and despair gets tumbled around my mind. Whatever I thought, whatever I dreamed of, this is it. This is him.

My father.

He runs over to me, silver eyes shining. "But look!" he says. "Your own storm, little Owl! You are kin! You are a new creature, in a world I thought incapable of change! Look, look down!"

Beneath my feet, and spreading fast around us both, is a fine layer of frost.

"So you have the basics," he says, nodding as he takes in my blue fingertips, the ice spreading up through my hair, making my scalp tight. "Now, come, take those boots off and be spirit. Come and play, little Owl!"

He whisks away again, as the North Wind comes back to the river. I sit and take off my boots, peeling off my socks and shaking my head at the madness of it all, while they howl at each other and throw handfuls of snow.

"Look!" Jack says, drawing the North Wind close to watch as I venture onto the ice, expecting my feet to sting with cold and feeling kind of amazed when they don't.

It feels like a marble floor, a little cool, a little slick, but perfectly manageable with bare feet. "Look at the little Owl! Is she not a wonderful creature? Look how small, how delicate her work!"

I look down as the North Wind comes closer. Fine swirls of ice are blooming with every footstep I take across the river, shining blue against the white. A shudder rolls down my spine and it's not all to do with the cold. This is the stuff dreams are made of, and it's really happening, right now, to *me*.

"Child," the North Wind says, coming closer, holding out his arms, throwing my hair back with his power. "Welcome."

I look back at him, feeling so uncertain and so elated at the same time, and he laughs with a bellow that sends a flurry of snow into my face.

"Ah, Jack," he cries. "She is wonderful! How did you find her?"

"She appeared last night," Jack says, as they both watch me come toward them. I feel like a kid taking its first steps, the way they're looking at me. I look down, focusing on the patterns spiraling away from my feet. "I think I shall take her under my wing. . . ."

I look up, my heart pounding, and the North Wind stares more closely as I reach them, his wide blue eyes bright as a summer sky in his round, timeless face.

"Spirit . . . and human?" He speaks as if to himself, his brow furrowing. "Ah, Jack . . ." He sighs, a blast of cold air dancing with the still falling snow. "The Royal Court will not like it. They already watch you closely."

Jack snorts, but the North Wind's eyes are full of doubt as he stares at me and I cannot hide. He seems to see straight to the heart of me.

"I think there is trouble here," he says eventually. "You are a wonderful creature indeed, child, but you are stepping in places not meant for humans. You are seeing things few have seen before. I do not know how it works . . . Jack, will you really encourage her? She should go home, be with her own kind."

"Her own kind cannot do these things!" Jack retorts. "My friend, you are worrying overmuch."

The North Wind gives another great sigh that catches me with yet another faceful of soft snow, and then he turns to the hills in the distance and runs toward them with great thundering steps, taking the sting of winter wind with him.

"So what do you do with yourself, little Owl?" Jack asks me, and I wonder if I like him calling me that. It's halfway between an endearment and teasing, the way he says it.

I shrug. "I go to school. Have friends. Occasionally freeze something . . ."

His eyes brighten. "That is the interesting part!"

"I quite like the rest of it, actually," I retort without thinking.

"You do not like to be like this?" he asks, gesturing at my frost-covered skin. I look at it. It is kind of beautiful: a tracery of delicate veins that shimmer in the pale light of the moon, gathering intricately over my knuckles and down my fingers. Beautiful, but not human. Not normal at all.

"I don't know," I say. "I'm not used to it. I'm used to being a normal girl, doing all the normal things. Seeing my friends, doing my homework, drawing . . ."

"Ah! To draw! Yes, that is a wonderful thing—to leave your mark behind as you go, yes. But can you touch—like this?" He leaps up to the river path and reaches out to the nearest tree, a spindly old ash, and draws a line of frost over the top of one of its branches. "Can you do that?"

He watches as I reach out tentatively. Calling upon it like this is very different. I haven't actually tried to do it deliberately before. My frost isn't like his. It comes and goes. It stutters and pulls at me, and as soon as it is there it disappears again, leaving me light-headed and dry-mouthed and a little ashamed.

"It's a worthy start." Jack nods. "Now, can you run, little Owl? Can you keep up with me?"

He sprints up the path toward the canal, frost spreading as he goes, and I follow, through the snow and over the frigid ground. And, honestly, I was never really into the whole sports thing, but this—running with the elements full in my face and my hair standing on end with ice, watching Jack Frost coat everything in sight with sparkling white, and the frozen river glowing blue white beneath the full moon—this rush in my blood is something that I wouldn't change for all the world. It grows as we go, so that it is no longer a stuttering, nervous thing. It's powerful and magical, and it's more than that because it's *me*. It's everything I have within me, everything I never imagined I could be.

23

Saturday morning is a bit lazy and I guess I'm happy with that. Mom's gone out on a trek with some friends to soak up the winter spirit in the deepest glens, or something, and normally I'd see Mallory, but she hasn't gotten in touch with me so I'm trying my best to sleep it all off while thoughts and memories of yesterday crash over me, mingling with my dreams.

By the time I open the curtains in my room it's nearly noon. Pale sunlight makes shadows sharp on the pavements and any signs of my frost adventures with Jack last night have long since burned away. I watch for a while, doodling in my art book: spiral eyes of exhausted owls who scatter autumn leaves with their wings while shadows loom in the corners.

And that's when I see it.

A small, pale figure standing in the shadows opposite, staring up at me. It's only the size of a small child, but clearly not a child at all. It's completely hairless, its bony limbs too long for its body, its gray skin glinting in the daylight. Large, lamp-like eyes look straight at me. I force myself to keep on looking, though it sends a shiver over my skin. And then it grins, revealing those wicked sharp teeth I thought I'd imagined. I flinch away despite myself, and when I look again, it's gone.

"But it *was* something," I tell myself fiercely, dimly aware that the temperature of the room has dropped by a couple of degrees, that there is now frost on the inside of the windowpane.

"It was, it was," clacks the wooden owl on the bedpost.

I turn in shock and bend down to study it more closely. It blinks, making me start. Mom carved it into the bedpost when I was a kid and scared of the dark. It's supposed to be my guardian. And now it's speaking to me. Or my mind is playing tricks on me. Either way, there's *definitely* something weird going on, with carved creatures talking to me and fairy creatures following me.

"Okay," I say to myself, sitting on the edge of the bed. "So there's Jack. And the North Wind. And Avery, who wants me to be sensible. And there's a whole Royal Fay Court of Mother Earth. And these *things* watching me. Are they from the Royal Court? Are they keeping an eye on me, making sure I behave? What do they *want*?"

I look at the owl, demanding an answer, but it's silent.

There must be a reason they're watching me. And if I'm powerless to do anything about Jack, or anything else, then perhaps I can at least do something about that—before they turn me into a gibbering wreck.

I spend most of the day at the window, pretending to do homework, waiting to see another one of the creatures. Mom drags me out to the kitchen for dinner when she gets home. She's brought vegan turnovers back from the wilds, and she asks after Mallory. It makes me squirm a bit. I can't remember the last time we didn't speak for this long, but I say something about her spending time with her mom and try to put it to the back of my mind. I'll fix it when I know how. After that, our conversation is muted and I can tell she's itching to get back to work in the studio. She's got that distracted glaze in her eyes.

"Are you all right, my love?" she asks, as I finish drying dishes and fling the towel on to the hook. "You seem down. We were going to have that talk—shall I leave my work for now?"

"I'm just tired," I say with a smile. "I was going to read for a bit and have an early night. Can we talk another time?"

She looks at me appraisingly. "It'll keep." She nods.

"Go safely there in your dreams." She smiles, reaching forward and giving me a quick hug. I lean into her for a second, taking comfort in her warmth, and when I pull back I do feel a bit better, a bit more like I can deal with this, whatever it might be. *She* did, after all.

"Thanks, Mom."

I watch out the window till my eyes ache and I'm seeing monsters everywhere. I watch as cars pull in, pull out again, as my neighbors welcome guests with wide smiles, as two arch-backed cats have a standoff in the middle of the road. And then I see it, deep in the shadows, its lamp-like eyes glowing.

I move as stealthily as I can from the window, getting up from the desk slowly and sneaking out of the bedroom door. The light's still on upstairs and I creep through the rest of the apartment, letting myself out with a soft click on the front door and running down the steps to the main entrance where I hesitate, door cranked open, until I see the creature again. It scrabbles up onto a low wall, its eyes fixed on my window, and then scuttles down and off along the road, keeping to the shadows. I grit my teeth and sneak through the front garden and over the road, following when it turns into one of the back streets toward the park, steeling myself for discovery at any second.

"Hey!" comes a whisper, just as I get to the field, making me jump out of my skin. "What are you doing?"

I turn to see Avery coming toward me and flap at him, hissing at him to be quiet before the creature spots us. He's quick on his feet and looks like he's been running, his hair tousled, breath tight.

"What's wrong?" I whisper, pulling him into the shadows with me.

"Nothing. I felt bad. I shouldn't have left you with Jack last night." He shrugs. "But what are you doing *now*?"

"I'm following one of the creatures!"

"What?" His eyes bore into me.

"Look, over there!" I point at the little figure, now halfway up the massive oak tree, its glittering skin lit by the moon. "I was right. They *are* following me. I've decided to follow back, to find out why they keep spying on me!"

"That's not a very good idea!" he whispers, and even in the dark I can make out the scowl on his face.

"Why not? I'm not making it up, Avery. Look! What is that, even?" I point at the inhuman figure as it scuttles through the branches.

"It looks like a goblin, one of the Royal Court's servants. I guess they're more curious than I thought they'd be—elementals don't normally have children. Maybe they *have* been watching you."

"Well, I don't like being spied on. I want to know what they're saying about me," I tell him, shuffling forward as the creature begins to leap from tree to tree ahead of us. In the distance looms the Old Druid Wood, where Mallory and I used to go "camping" for an afternoon, our bags packed with potato chips and apples and flashlights. "You can either help me or go away. I'm fed up with sitting at home worrying about everything, not knowing what's going on."

Avery swears under his breath.

"What is it?" I demand, my eyes focused on the small figure still darting ahead. "Why are you so worried?"

"I'm not *worried*. It's late, and you're chasing ideas with no basis!"

"So don't come! It's fine, really. Just leave me to my lunacy, and I'll catch up with you at school. . . ." I wink at him and scurry forward, deeper into the little tangle of trees and toward the woodland, the goblin always just within sight. After a moment and with a low huff, Avery follows me and I am glad of it, though I'd never say that to him.

My breath is tight, and my skin feels a size too small for me. I'm aware that there's ice in the creases of my wrists and elbows and knees, that my hair is crusted with frost.

I crouch, ignoring it while Avery's breath steams in the air next to me. We found them. In a little clearing in the middle of the wood, where the trees are tightly knit and thrust their roots out to trip careless feet, suddenly the pale figure of the Royal Court servant was joined by two other, taller figures, whose features I can't make out in the darkness.

". . . We should just make our move, this is tedious, and I'll be out of my season before much longer. . . ." A man's voice, low and barbed with impatience. It sounds too deep to be that of the creature we followed.

"This is the long game, my dear friend," replies a woman's soft voice. "We must know all we can before we go any further. We need the sympathy of the whole Royal Court on our side."

"The goblins aren't bringing anything useful, and unless she's very stupid she's going to spot one at some point. I don't know why you insist upon them. She's . . ." There's a shifting of feet in the clearing and I try to peer through, but Avery is in the way and seemingly oblivious, caught up in it himself. He shuffles back as I get closer, thrusting me farther into a gnarly old bush. I miss whatever the man was going to say about me as I try to struggle out without making any noise. I glare at him in a "What are you doing?" outraged sort of way and he indicates the clearing, gesturing impatiently to his ears, and then his eyes, and putting a finger over his lips to shut me up. Not that I was going to say anything. I turn away from him and try to pick up their voices again.

". . . We'll need all the evidence we can find. It's no small thing we're attempting here. And before you start yowling again, remember we're in this together. We set the trap and now there's no escape, we have everything we need to destroy him. It's just a matter of timing. We want the same thing, after all—to be rid of Jack and his invasion upon our seasons with his infernal frost. She is key to all of it. Now, then, what have you for us today, Sparling?"

"She is keen-eyed, my Queen," comes a thin whisper. "And she has a guardian. I could not work out which. I caught a sense of it from the window. She has been active with Jack, out at night playing with their art. She is trusting. Humans are."

"Well, that will go in our favor, at least," says the Queen. "You see, dear friend? Your own project may well bear fruit! How does he fare?"

"I believe it is going well," replies the man. "I wonder if we should ask . . ."

Suddenly, after all his warnings to me about keeping quiet, Avery loses his balance and treads heavily, snapping the brittle, frozen twigs beneath our feet. A sudden bloom of silence seems to stretch around us. Avery looks at me, panic written all over his face. "Run!" he hisses, rushing toward me, grabbing me by the arm and pulling me through whipping branches and over the frozen ground until we are back out on the park. He doesn't stop there, either. His feet fly, and mine are forced to follow, stumbling, breath like fire in my lungs, until we're back in the well-lit suburban streets around the park.

"What happened?" I demand when we finally stop. I pull away from him and lean up against a fence, heart pounding.

"I'm sorry," he says with a wince, bending to recover his breath. "My foot went numb, and I knew they'd have heard me crashing about. I didn't want us to get caught."

"But they were just about to say something important, I know they were!" I sigh and try to let go of the frustration. It wasn't really his fault. "Who were they? One of them was a queen!"

"The Queen of May," he says. "I'm not sure what she's trying to achieve with all this, but she's a schemer, and she's not a fan of Jack. Spring versus winter, I suppose."

"Who was the man with her?" I shudder at the memory of his harsh, uncaring voice.

"Don't know," says Avery, closing his eyes and leaning his head back against the fence. "I've no idea what they're all doing."

"Well, they're trying to get rid of Jack! I'll have to warn him."

"Do you really have to?" he asks. "What's he done for you, Owl? How do you know it wouldn't all be better without him?"

"Do you think it would be? What's he done that's so wrong anyway?" I ask.

"He's too wild. Some say he's forgotten why he does what he does. He's destructive."

"But he's Jack Frost! How can you get rid of him? Isn't he just being what he should be, doing his work?"

"I'm not getting involved," he says, shaking his head. "And if I were you, I'd stay out of it."

I watch him walk away, slope-shouldered but still tall, and somehow incongruous against the pale dawn, his tawny hair like a burning challenge to winter itself.

24

FABLES & EARTH SPIRITS

The Queen of May

It was a paradise, and she was entranced by it. The sky was endless blue, and the air rang with the chatter of small, bright birds. Green fields stretched out in every direction, tiny flowers of every color nestled like stars within their folds. The girl's heart soared to see such a place, and then the mistress of it all appeared before her and she was caught by the desolation in those green eyes, by the yearning that gleamed there.

"What creature are you, to come before me thus?" the lady hissed, porcelain skin flushed red with rage as she looked her up and down. "How do you DARE to appear

here without invitation?"

"I am . . . I am just—"

"STOP stammering! Thou art like a frightened child." The lady thrust her hands out as if the girl's presence caused her pain, her blossom-pink hair swirling about her face. She took a deep breath: the world around them seemed to dim and contract, and then all blazed forth once more, green and bountiful. New life was everywhere here, from the buds on the trees to the baby rabbits that bounced around them. Small figures giggled in the shade of rose bushes and for a moment the girl wondered if they were children, but they were not. Their skin was palest gray, their little teeth serrated—they were nothing human at all.

"Do not be afraid," the lady said then with a sudden, bright smile that made the girl's head swim. "You catch me out of season, it is a hard time for me."

"Out of season?"

"I am the Queen of May—I am SPRING!" she howled, stamping a bare foot as clouds gathered in the cornflower sky. Her fists clenched at her sides, the skirt of her dress swirling out in a sudden wind. "You come to me when your world is stuck in the depths of bitter winter and expect to find me WELCOMING?"

"No, I . . . Forgive me. I did not know where I was, I only sought to—"

"To what? To torture me with reminders of a world where I am not welcome? You tread daily on the solid earth, you have no limits, no bounds, and I am here with only what I create for company, TRAPPED until my season rings once more. Does it seem fair to you? DOES it?"

Her voice rose to a screech and the creatures around them froze, their eyes fixed on the girl accusingly. "Fix this," they seemed to say. "You have spoiled our play with your wretched humanity."

"N-no, my lady, please . . ."

The girl twisted her hands and wished herself away, but it did not work. She had never been able to discover the trick of leaving these places at will. The sky darkened, and then it was as if the Queen grew bored of her temper once more. Her countenance changed entirely, and the world brightened with her.

"Come," she said presently, sweeping to a bench tucked away in a bower of sweet-smelling honeysuckle. She sat and gazed about with another dazzling, intoxicating smile. "Come, my goblin friends, gather . . . come, human! I shall tell you tales of my season on the earth. That shall cheer us all."

The girl never did know how long she was in that paradise. The time is ever different when one is abroad with the fay. It felt like half a lifetime, and she grew almost fond of the mischievous goblins that courted their lady and made her laugh with their spiteful little tricks. But as for the fickle Queen of May—she would be very glad if she never saw her like again.

25

"Owl!" Mallory whispers as she opens her front door. "What are you doing?"

It's early morning already and I'm exhausted and disoriented. My feet found their own way here; I'm almost as surprised as she is to find myself on her doorstep.

"Your mom is freaking out! And why don't you have a coat on? You've got bare arms! Out in the snow!"

She's making my head ache with all the exclamation marks.

"Can I come in?"

She looks toward the kitchen, where the radio is on, and puts her finger to her lips before pulling me in and hustling me up the stairs. Nice, soft carpet, nice warm house. The familiar smell of baking. Now that I'm here, I don't know where to start—there's so much to fill her in on, and that's if she wants to hear it.

"Sorry about before," I mumble as we get into her room. I crawl up onto her bed. Nice, clean, warm blankets, lots of pillows. Mallory has a nice room. Little cherries on the wallpaper, everything clean and white and organized in plastic files on polished shelves.

"It's okay," she says in a small voice. "I'm sorry, too." She lingers in the doorway, as if she doesn't know whether to stay or go. She's wearing pajamas with cupcakes on them.

"Sure you don't mind me coming over?" I ask eventually through the strained silence.

"No! I don't know!" she says. "Where've you been all night anyway? Everyone's been in a panic, Owl. Are you okay? You have to tell me what's *really* going on—I can't cope with you getting all distant." She blinks hard. "Everything's falling apart," she whispers. "Mom and Dad are having all these tense phone conversations, and you're keeping things from me, and I know that's up to you and you've got your own stuff, but it doesn't feel . . . nothing feels the same anymore!"

I pull her down next to me on the bed.

"I'm sorry," I say, watching her struggle not to cry, feeling awful because I've been so absorbed in my stuff that I haven't really thought about how everything has changed for her, not properly. "I'm sorry about your mom and dad. I'm sorry I haven't been here for you—"

"Stop!" she says firmly, taking a deep breath and turning to face me. "I've had enough of talking about me. Tell me what's going on with you."

I struggle for a minute, all the events of the last couple of days piling up in my mind, confusing everything. Then I decide to start at the beginning and go from there. Honestly, I'm not sure how much of this madness she'll be able to take, anyway. I've never seen her so fragile.

"I found my father," I say.

Her face lights up. "You did? Tell me! What's he like?"

"He's a bit . . . He's not quite the usual. I mean . . . He's Jack Frost," I blurt.

She grins. "Ha-ha, nice one. Did she really tell you, or are you just trying to distract me from all my own stuff?"

"Uh . . ." I look down at the pale carpet, wondering what to say next. I can't think of anything. "I'm not kidding, Mall. . . ."

"So your father is Jack Frost?" She peers at me and I lift my head, trying not to react. Trying to fend off the shudder in my spine, the rush of ice behind my eyes. "*The* Jack Frost? As in . . . kids' stories? You're really telling me, in total seriousness, that your mom says *he* is your father?"

"Yes!" I breathe, a little flurry of ice escaping my mouth as I say it.

She flinches back, eyes wide.

"But how is that . . ."

"Mallory!" Her mom's voice, her footsteps on the stairs. "What's going on? Who do you have in there?"

I huddle into the corner of the bed and pull a pillow over my face.

"Uh, wait a minute," says Mallory, shaking her head. "I'll get Mom to call yours, let her know you're here."

"I'm not going home yet," I say, dreading the thought of facing Mom.

"I'll see what I can do," she says. "Anyway, I want to know what's going on with you before you go anywhere." She looks at me, cowering behind the pillow, and shakes her head again. "I'll get us some tea. You must be half frozen."

"I *am* half frozen!" I crow, bursting out into a weird, gasping laughter that tears at my throat.

"Oh God, Owl, what am I going to do with you? Just . . . let me get the tea and then we'll work it out."

I love Mallory.

I close my eyes, and wake with a start when she comes back in with two steaming mugs of tea and a plate of toasted bagels. I watch her clatter about for a bit and try to clear my mind of dreams. They dance before my eyes still: old men with blue eyes, snow in my face and skating on ice, frost sweeping across rooftops all at the touch of a finger, my father's face, his expression always slightly mocking, and strange figures, leading me onto thin ice where Avery waits for me.

"So . . . Jack Frost," Mallory says eventually, sitting on the bed, her eyes flicking over me.

"Yup."

"And this is what you've been hiding?"

I nod. "I didn't know how to tell you."

"I suppose that's not surprising," she says, grabbing a bagel and pulling her laptop over. She peers at me, frowning. "Not if you really believe your father is Jack Frost."

I try to explain what he's like as the mug of tea warms me from the inside. I'm so disoriented I do a really bad job of it. I keep stumbling over words and forgetting things and having to go back and fill bits in. To Mallory's credit she just sits and listens, and though her eyes boggle a bit, she doesn't laugh again or tell me I'm mad. Her tea goes cold, the bagel still in her hand, forgotten, as I try to make her understand.

"Well?" I ask, when I'm done telling her about him and what I've learned about the fay world, searching her face for clues. "What do you think?"

She purses her lips, looking out of the window at the frozen world, now gleaming beneath a clear sky.

"Do you think I'm making it all up?"

"No," she says in a subdued voice. "I know you were

out all night, and that you arrived not looking in the slightest bit cold. And something's been up with your body temperature, and all the sparkling. And, you know, your mom's stories . . . and then you are called Owl." She peers at me, her eyes troubled. "Maybe we should google Jack Frost, see if we can find out more about him."

"I already did. It's just a load of nonsense."

"Well, I'm doing it, anyway. Maybe there'll be something you missed that can explain it all somehow," she says.

I grab one of the bagels, closing my eyes while she starts tapping away. She's humoring me, I can tell. Maybe she thinks I'm losing it and she's playing along in case I freak out altogether. I guess I can't really blame her.

"Hmm, there is a load of nonsense," she says after a few minutes. "But also some good stuff . . ." She reads me an old poem about Jack Frost icing windows and lakes, making the world all beautiful, and then destroying a bowl of fruit and a pitcher—which sounds about right.

"The North Wind was there too," I mumble, opening my eyes to see her now scrolling through images of white-haired boys who don't look a bit like my father. "Did I say?"

"Yes, of course he was," she says, shooting me a quizzical look. "Let's focus on your dad for now though, shall we? One mythical creature at a time?"

"'Kay."

Mallory's mom pops her head around the door. "I've spoken to your mom," she says, tucking her hair behind her ears. She looks a bit tired, but apart from that she's as pristine as ever, just like the house. I wonder what it'd be like to have a mom like that, parents like Mallory's. "I told her you're here safe. . . ."

"Thank you."

"She's been very worried, Owl. She's expecting you home before too long,"

"Okay," I whisper, looking down.

"At least she knows where you are now," she says, looking from me to Mallory.

"She's being nice to me. She thinks that can make up for everything else," Mallory says when she's disappeared, closing the door behind her.

"Oh, Mall . . ."

She waves a hand and turns back to the computer, and I get it—she wants to get absorbed in something else, anything but what's going on with her mom and dad. So we're back into Jack Frost. There's a Norse legend about a frost giant, and in some cultures he's also known as Old Man Winter. Then we look up what frost is good for. There's not a lot of evidence it's good for anything, actually, just lots about frost being bad for gardeners and fruit.

"So, basically, he's an inhuman creature who goes

around killing tomatoes and causing trouble for people," I say, folding my arms and leaning back against the wall. "Sounds about right, really. He's not terribly . . . warm." Mallory snorts. "No. But I mean, in the kind way. He's a bit of a joker."

"Well, but you don't know him yet, do you? Not just from one night . . ." She frowns at me, then takes a deep breath and turns back to the computer. "Anyway, isn't there also something about frost protecting earth from winter? I'm sure . . . I mean, everything in nature has a purpose, doesn't it?"

She's a bit of an environmentalist, Mallory. She can't find anything to back it up, though.

"What difference does it make, anyway?" I ask in the end. "I mean, what kind of relationship can you have with Jack Frost? He just spends all his time running around, freezing things, not really caring about anything."

"Maybe that's the point," she says with an impatient shrug. "Maybe you could make him care, Owl."

"And then what?"

"I don't know! Then you'd have a dad who cares!" Her eyes sparkle with sudden tears.

"*Your* dad cares!"

"I know," she says fiercely, thrusting the computer aside and pulling a pillow onto her lap. "I just wish he'd come home."

❄❄❄

"What's with you and Avery, then?" she asks later, when we've reached the lemonade-and-cookies portion of the day and I've been told very firmly by her mother that I can't keep hiding here. Mom is expecting me home for dinner.

"He's connected with, uh, with the fay world," I say, a little niggle of tension writhing in my belly as she frowns. "He's been helping me to work it all out, and then I was following one of the fay creatures, and he found me and insisted on coming with me."

"Coming with you where? What fay creature?" Her eyes bore into me and I shift uneasily.

"I don't know. . . . Some kind of servant of the Royal Court of Mother Earth—a goblin, I think. I wanted to find out why they've been following me."

"Following you? Someone's been following you? Why didn't you say before?" She frowns. "Why are you putting all your trust in Avery? We don't know him, Owl! He only started at the school a week ago!"

My throat feels dry. I've got this wrong somehow. I didn't realize the Avery thing would be such a big deal.

"He grew up in that world and I . . . I needed to know anything he could tell me. Maybe I should have told you earlier, I just . . . I don't know! I never meant to shut you out, Mall!"

"Everyone does, all the same," she says in a stony voice. "Mom, Dad . . . and you." She looks sick, and in spite of my own anger my stomach lurches, because I know I have let her down just when she needed me. Mallory's not a drama queen, she doesn't very often actually want much at all. I should have done more. Been around more for her.

"I'm sorry. . . ."

She flinches, like she's heard it all before. "It's fine. I get it. But you should go home now. This isn't getting us anywhere, and your mom will be worrying." She gets up and opens the door, all flushed and bright-eyed.

"Mallory!"

"Really, it's fine," she says. "I need to spend some time with Mom anyway. We'll talk at school."

She doesn't look at me, and I don't know what to say to make it better. In the end I have no choice but to leave. I stumble down the smooth, carpeted stairs, past her mother without a word, my head reeling, fingers fumbling with the door latch before finally it yields and I'm back out in the cold, wondering what I should have said, whether there was anything I *could* have said that would have made it all seem okay to her.

I hate fighting with Mallory. It's all we seem to do since I found out about Jack.

26

As soon as I let myself into the apartment there are footsteps pounding on the wooden stairs that lead to the studio, and then Mom comes hurtling around the corner, flying into me, spattering ocher paint everywhere as she goes.

"Owl!"

"Mom! What is it?"

She pulls back. She looks tired and pale, even more disheveled than usual, a gray sweater thrown on over her pajamas, all of it sprinkled with ocher and a deep vermilion color.

"*What is it?*" She shakes her head. "My girl! One day you will know what real fear is like, perhaps. And then you will know how I felt when you didn't come home! Where were you, Owl? What were you doing?"

She's half wild with energy, not exactly angry, but pretty intense all the same.

"I'm sorry," I say as she herds me into the kitchen, flicking on the lamp on the old dresser and perching up on the side, watching me. Paint drips from the brush on to the old floor tiles but she doesn't notice. "I did go to Mallory's, honestly. But before that, I went out with . . . with a different friend . . ."

"Who?"

"His name's Avery—"

"A boy?" Her voice rises with disbelief.

"Yes, a boy!" I feel a bit outraged at her reaction. I might be lying a bit, but it's pretty much the truth. And what's so surprising about me being with a boy, anyway?

"And who is *Avery*?" she asks, narrowing her eyes.

"He's new! We just met by an old tree and talked. That's all!"

Oh, this is not going well. What a stupid thing to say. My mind is still reeling from my fight with Mallory. I hardly know what's going to come out of my mouth next.

"Avery," she murmurs. "There's meaning in a name like that, bound to be."

"Maybe his mom just liked it," I retort. "And you've got paint all over the floor."

She tuts and shakes her head, whether at me or herself I'm not sure. I grab the paper towels and help her tidy it up, after which she starts pulling things out of the fridge—cheese, hummus, carrot sticks—and handing them to me. She's made little seed cookies and commands me to put them on a plate while she makes miso soup in big mugs, stirring too hard while I watch, feeling a bit nervous. She's preparing for a lecture: I can tell from the flare of her nostrils. She loves a good lecture. They usually make perfect sense, even when repeated five times over.

"And so . . . " she says, once we've sorted everything and settled at the kitchen table, taking a deep breath as she looks me up and down. "Owl, I cannot trust you if you lie to me like that. Did you think I would stop you?"

"I don't know. I just didn't want to say anything." I grab a seed cookie.

"You're growing up, and I'm trying to understand. But the lying, and the staying out—you're still too young for that, Owl."

"I'm sorry," I say through a spray of seeds. Wow, these cookies are like compressed grit.

"I know you are," she says in a tight voice. "But it isn't . . ." She tips her head back, drumming her fingers on the table. When she looks back at me her eyes are glittering, her jaw tense. "It doesn't change anything. It's the second time in a week. And you lied to me. You went out, and I didn't know where you were or when you'd be home. I didn't know you were safe!"

"I . . ."

"No." She shakes her head. "No, this is my time for talking, Owl. You're special, we both know that. And we don't know what that will bring in time. But for now you are *my* girl, and I will keep you safe for as long as I can." She hesitates, takes a deep breath. "You're grounded."

"Mom!"

"What did you expect?" she demands. "There are consequences, Owl, to everything. This is the consequence. You're grounded for one week, at least."

I've never been grounded before. I never thought I would be.

I suppose lots of things have happened in the last week that I never expected.

"It just . . . doesn't seem fair," I sigh to the owl on the bedpost later as I open my bag and haul the books out.

"Fair, fair," comes a whisper through the room, making my ears ring. I look at the wooden owl and around at all the others up on the walls. They're silent, not a flutter between them, and I almost wish they *would* come alive and talk to me, because I'm not sure I've ever felt so alone. I try to get a grip on my math homework, but the loops and whirls of algebra suddenly look like Jack's frost patterns on the windows, and I get lost again, thinking about last night and the plot against him. I'll have to tell him. Not tonight, but soon. I picture him out there, stalking the streets and covering them with silver-white ice. Then I imagine myself out there with him, and I know I won't be able to wait for long.

27

FABLES & EARTH SPIRITS

The Earl of October

It was a flurry and a riot, in that place, and for a moment she hardly knew which was up, which was down. Golden leaves spun in the air, rustled underfoot and drifted every which way, carried on a mild wind. She ran like a child, kicking into the chaos—she could not help herself. But she should have, for the Earl of October *is zealous in his rule.*

"What do you do here?" he screamed at her, stalking down a long, tree-lined avenue, the leaves turning red as he passed. "What do you seek? Humanity has no place in my kingdom!"

He was an awesome sight: half as tall as the tallest tree, his skin like bark. His limbs were knobby, his hair like nothing more than the curling, twisted roots that crept beneath their feet.

The girl turned and ran.

It was the first, the only time she had ever done so. She had faced far more spiteful creatures, even far more dangerous, but there are few in the world who bear the rage of the Earl of October. And there are few who look so monstrous.

28

I wake to the sound of glass being clawed at, a horrible, thin, tortured sound that makes my ears ache. My breath plumes as I turn my head and look toward the window, a small cloud of ice particles forming in the air.

What is that?

The sound comes again, and then there's a tap. Small but insistent. I shuffle out of bed and lift the curtain to peek out, little prickles of fear running up my spine.

There's an owl drawn in ice on the window: intricate and beautiful, its wings outspread, eyes fierce and determined as it looks to the ground. It reflects the moonlight and glints, so real looking I can't help but reach out a hand to touch it.

And then Jack looms out of the darkness, a wicked smile on his face as he leans out from the silver birch that stands in the garden. He beckons. I shake my head, though I can already feel the adrenaline building in my blood. He frowns and reaches out, knocks against the glass a little harder, a little louder. I shake my head more vigorously, but he just raises his eyebrows and knocks again.

"Stop it!" I hiss, terrified that Mom might hear and come in. I mean, what would that be like? Apart from her discovering that I've lied to her far more than she realizes, she'd be face-to-face with Jack Frost for the first time in over thirteen years. I have no idea how that would go. She's always been so accepting of what happened, the fact that she would never see him again, but if she *did* see him that would change, wouldn't it? And then what? There's a part of me, a small, selfish part, that wants to keep him to myself, just for now.

Jack begins to fling small pellets of ice at the window, just below the owl.

"What do you want?" I mouth at him, another cloud of ice forming in front of my face.

He grins. "Come out," he mouths. "I want to show you something."

I grab my boots and my hat and creep down the hall to the front door. All's in darkness. Mom's not working tonight. I feel a horrible twinge of guilt grip me, deep in my belly, and I loiter for a moment in the tiny hall, looking at Mom's paintings of stags and wolves hanging on the walls. Animals of winter, their stance wary, eyes defiant, as they roam in frozen wilderness. She saw those creatures when she was with my father, I realize suddenly. They were in the stories. It's time. Time for me to know him for myself.

I grab my keys from the shelf and shut the door behind me, pulling on my boots and treading down the steps to the main door as softly as I can. I take my time to unbolt it and venture, coatless, into the cold November night, my father landing lightly on his feet as he jumps from the tree to meet me.

"Come, little pretender," he says, whisking me out of the gate and leading me down the silent, dark road. "You say you like to sketch. Let's see how well you do with my tricks—"

"Jack, wait," I interrupt, looking around for the pale shadowy figure who's been spying on me. The road is still, nothing moves. "Something's been spying on me. There's a plot against you."

"A plot?" He spins around, searching the shadows, little flurries of ice dancing in the air around him, sparking golden beneath the streetlight. "Tell me more!" He looks delighted.

"The Queen of May and someone else. I don't know who. They're trying to be rid of you. . . ."

"Be rid of me! What a delightful notion! I am Jack Frost, little Owl, they cannot be rid of me so easily as that!"

"But they've been watching me, they— "

"Now, little Owl," he says. "This is the night. This is the time for magic. Come away from all these petty concerns. They do not worry me in the slightest! Come—I will show you how to make this home of yours a more beautiful place!"

And he does. He changes the world with every step he takes. With every gesture, the winter wonderland Mom spoke of seems to come alive around us, so that every house becomes a sparkling palace, every street a sweep of dazzling white that catches the starlight and glistens. Jack bounds from pavement to streetlight, over fences and up the narrow, skeletal trees, and at his every touch magic spreads. He's wide-eyed and intent on his work, a dart of silver throwing spears of mirror-bright ice up into the eaves of every building, spirals that wink and glitter. My feet fly after his, my blood pumping faster, colder through my veins until I am as lost to it as he is, freezing ponds with a touch of my finger, lacing windows in a fine pale crystal fur. I don't know how far we go—I lose track of the real world after a while, so that the streets that I have trodden all my life are a million miles away. This is his domain, and it is my domain, and it is more beautiful than I could ever have imagined.

❄❄❄

The night gets deeper, more silent around us as we work, never speaking but connected with every action, and I am wired with this magic, a flutter of pride going through me every time he looks approvingly at what I've done . . . but gradually exhaustion begins to creep in. We skirt the school and head through some community gardens, and for a while I'm caught up making tiny fern patterns on the greenhouses, but when I turn around, Jack is leaning down, his fingers reaching through the gaps in the protective plastic the gardeners have put over the ground, a fine bloom of ice instantly taking the life out of the vegetables nestled underneath. Something catches within me, the memory of my argument with Mallory stings, and the spell is broken.

"No!" I protest. "Why would you do that?"

"It's nature," he says, looking up with a smile. "It's part of the cycle of the world, little Owl."

"But it's cruel! Is it really necessary?"

"How else does the world know that it is time to shelter from the winter?"

But I see the light in his eyes as he does it: he enjoys it. It's like a little act of rebellion or spite. When Mom talked about him, she always made him sound so wise and gentle, despite his strangeness and the treachery of winter. I hadn't imagined that he could be like this here.

My footsteps are heavy as I follow him to neighboring gardens, rushing along the spikes of a wooden fence, frost cascading from his touch down to the ground.

Suddenly there's a commotion in the darkness at the edge of the garden. Trees rustle wildly, and a tall, broad figure appears, stretching up to his full height. He's nearly as high as the tip of the garden shed, I see with shock as he unfolds himself—he must be at least seven feet tall.

"Jack!" he barks, his voice hard as granite.

I recognize that voice. I take a step back, trying to hide my shock, and Jack leaps down from the fence.

"Ah, bother," Jack says, rising to his full height, still dwarfed by the other man. "What is it now, you old grump?" He stands straight and square, and beckons for me to join him. I swallow a niggle of fear and edge up, standing slightly behind him, looking up into the stern face of a man more peculiar by far even than my father: the man who spoke with the Queen last night. I try to find my voice, try to warn Jack, but nothing will come. The man has pale, mottled skin like the bark of a silver birch. His eyes are wide and brown, and they would be beautiful, but the expression in them is so hard they only remind me of the knots in wood. His body is long and lean, his limbs gnarled, his hair a riot of oranges and reds and copper browns.

"Who is this?" he asks, stooping with a creak to

inspect me. His sharp teeth are gray, his breath bittersweet, like rotting fruit. I shudder despite myself, and his hollow eyes gleam. "Who is this creature, Jack, that you share your antics with?"

"She is of no concern to you!" Jack snaps. "Only a sprite, that's all."

"A sprite, you say? Do you think me stupid? That is no sprite, Jack."

"Why are you here?" Jack demands, squaring up to the man. "This is not your domain."

"Autumn stretches far longer than you have ever allowed for," the man says with a tight smile. "As long as you dance through the fallen amber leaves of my doing I may remain abroad, Jack. It is you who must account for things."

"I need not explain myself to you," Jack says firmly, folding his arms.

"Very well," says the man. "Then you may come to the Royal Court. On the twenty-first, Jack, two days from now. Midnight." He reaches out and touches Jack on the forehead with a long, gnarled finger. "You have been summoned."

Jack leaps back, outraged, shoving me backward. I fall easily, all my strength giving out at the appearance of this new figure. Jack curses and reaches out a hand, and I notice it shakes as it grips mine. "Up!" he says. "Do not fall before these creatures. . . .”

But when we look around, the man has gone.

“And there was the Earl of October,” Jack says in a dry tone. “Embittered by lack of power and prestige, far too concerned with human notions of respect.”

“But it was him, Jack! He was the one plotting against you with the Queen. And now he’s seen us together—won’t that be bad? I should have said something when he was here. . . . Are you in trouble because of me?”

He looks surprised.

“Well. That is interesting. I wonder what he thinks he has over me.” He looks in the direction the Earl left and gives a shrug. “Ah, I am in trouble several times a year. It is nothing I cannot deal with. Now, come, little Owl, ’tis nearly time for your human day to start.”

Whatever he may say, the encounter has shifted something in him. He’s silent as we walk home, keeping to the shadows as a leaden dawn begins to break. He salutes me good-bye at the door as I step inside, and when I look back to watch him walk away, his head is lowered, his footsteps barely more than a mist on the ground.

At least something is going my way. I manage to get myself back into the apartment and into bed without alerting Mom. There seems a lot to worry about, but each little thing is like a darting minnow: I can’t get hold of anything to consider it properly.

I've never known before quite what it meant to be bone tired.

It means you're bone tired.

As in: every bone.

Tired.

29

When I wake it's after eleven. Mom's put a cup of tea down by the bed and when I reach out it's still warm. I sit up, pulling the curtains aside and huddling into the quilt, drinking my tea, watching the sun make the frost sparkle on the rooftops opposite. The owl on the window is no longer there, I realize with a little pang. Everything Jack does is so temporary.

I drag my laptop down from the desk and look up sprites. Of all the things that have happened, it's the bit that sticks with me. Jack said it so dismissively: she's "only a sprite."

Mostly the word has been hijacked by the soft drink. I scroll down impatiently and find this definition:

A small, otherworldly figure mentioned in folklore; part of the "fay" or "fairy" domain.

I suppose that's not such an insult. And I know he was only saying it to cover his tracks. But why was the Earl of October so pleased to have caught him out? What can they do to him, for being found with a half human?

A half human.

I look down at myself.

A human with extras. That's what I am.

Mom takes me out for a walk. I feel like a dog called to heel. She watches me closely the whole time as we trudge through the browning snow, heading for the canal. All too clearly I can see the traces of my father's antics last night, and in some of the patterns in the river I can even see my own. Mom tries to start a conversation several times but I'm too tired and distracted, and eventually she gives up, putting her arm through mine instead. I let it stay there, then we go to Mallory's on the way home, so my mom can catch up with hers, which is a bit awkward, since Mallory and I are not exactly on speaking terms. She stares at me across the hallway for a moment, while our mothers head to the kitchen, and I stare back, folding my arms. I know I made mistakes, not telling her things sooner, but she was the one who threw me out.

Eventually she sighs and gestures to the stairs.

"You look even more tired than yesterday," she hisses as I trail behind her. She manages to look concerned and furious at the same time when she glances back. "You should slow down a bit." She reaches out and pulls me up the last few stairs. "I mean, I'm sorry if it sounds harsh, Owl. I'm just trying to look out for you!"

"I know you are," I answer, closing her bedroom door behind us, hearing the soft murmur of our mothers talking downstairs. "I get it. I just don't know what I can do about it. I mean, do you want to know stuff, or not? I can't have another argument, I'm too tired."

"I can see that," she says, sitting with me on the bed, her fingers absently playing with the hem of her T-shirt. "No more arguments. What have you been up to this time?"

I tell her about the Earl of October and the plot against Jack and the summons to the Royal Court. Her eyes get brighter as I talk, and I don't know whether she truly believes it all, but she's always loved a good adventure, in spite of her more sensible self, and suddenly I know just how to fix everything between us.

"So this Royal Court thing, that's tomorrow night?" she asks when I've finished.

"Yup." I take a deep breath and plunge ahead. "Do you want to come? I need to go, just in case I can help Jack.

I might be the only one who knows about this plot. . . . Avery told me they meet in the Old Druid Wood. I don't know quite where, but I'll get Avery to tell me and then we can go together."

"With Avery?"

Sheesh.

"I don't know, that's not the point! Do *you* want to come, or not?"

"Yes, definitely," she says, biting her lip.

"What's the problem then?"

"It's just . . . it's hard for me to imagine it all! Is this really happening, Owl? If you're really Jack Frost's daughter, what does that actually *mean*?"

I close my eyes and think of last night, out with Jack, how the power builds inside and then unfurls slowly. I focus on the tingling in my arms and legs, feel it sweep out all around me.

When I open my eyes Mallory is open-mouthed with shock, and the bed is a moon-bright ship on a sea of frost, great jagged shards of ice sweeping up all around us almost to the ceiling. The quilt is a deck of pale, frozen flowers that gleam beneath the bedroom light, which has been transformed into a shimmering chandelier. Tier after tier of clear, sparkling ice scatters the light in a thousand rainbow reflections, and glittering crystals hang down, tinkling gently.

"Owl!" Mallory chokes eventually, after what seems like hours.

"You wanted to see!" I whisper, as the feeling gets stronger and the ceiling begins to creak, icicles forming over our heads.

"Yes, but . . . but . . ." She reaches forward and picks up one of the flowers, her eyes like saucers as she holds it in her hand. "But look at this! Look at you!"

"It's only me," I say, tears stinging in my eyes before spilling into my lap. "I mean, I thought you knew. . . ."

"Yes! I know, it's just . . . I'm sorry, I didn't mean to make you . . . It's awesome! Can you stop it?" she asks, her voice breathless, wiping her hand on her leg as the flower melts. "I mean—" she looks up at the twisting, spear-like icicles "—maybe before they fall?"

I have to concentrate really hard to let the feeling go. It feels like I'm winding in a web of needle-sharp silver, trying to contain something that doesn't want to be contained at all. It takes more effort than it did to show her in the first place. The frost doesn't disappear for a while either, and I feel this strange mixture of pride and desperation, because that feeling, when I'm doing it, that feeling is like pure joy and now I'm without it. Now I'm just sitting here being stared at by my best friend while ice melts around us.

"So?" I ask after a while, my voice shaking.

"I get it," she says. "I think I get it."

"Are you coming then?"

"Yes!" she says, running a finger through the frost on her headboard. "Will your mom let you, after the other night?"

"No," I say. "I'll have to sneak out. Are you up for that?"

"Absolutely," she says. "But what's wrong? You look awful. . . ."

"It's tiring," I say. "And you staring like that makes me feel weird. Also, I've kind of made your room wet. . . ."

"Oh, it'll be okay, I'll chuck some towels around in a bit," she says. "Don't worry about that. And I'm sorry for staring—it's not because it's weird, Owl, it's because it's magical!"

I snort. She sounds like a five-year-old. Then she shoves me and I shove her back, and we're laughing and we're us again, even if the conversation is different now.

I just hope it's the right thing to take her. I know it's the right thing for me, for our friendship. I'm just not sure how good it'll be for Jack. I mean, if he's in trouble for hanging out with a half human, how's he going to fare if I take a whole one along with me for his Royal Court appearance?

We make our plans anyway, and then the subject strays on to Mallory's parents and I see how desperate she is about them, how hard she's trying to lose herself in other stuff because there's nothing she can do to fix their problems. It'll be good for her to come. If I can get Avery to tell me where the Royal Court meets, that is.

Avery still looks tired when he walks into homeroom in the morning. He gives me a quick half smile before marching over and sitting at his usual desk, glaring at Conor when he arrives and starts being deliberately annoying, flapping his coat around and taking an age to sit down.

"Avery doesn't look very happy, does he?" Mallory whispers as Mr. Varley bursts into the room and starts shouting at Conor for being a clown. Conor is unfazed as usual. He just grins and takes his seat, and then he looks across and winks at Mallory, who goes a very interesting shade of pink.

"Ooh, Conor's happy to see you, though," I say with a grin.

She raps me on the knuckle with a pencil.

I can feel Avery's gaze boring into me for the whole of class, though every time I turn around he's looking straight ahead at Mr. Varley. I loiter outside the classroom when the bell has gone, waiting for him.

"Hi," I say, standing in his way.

He looms over me. "Hi."

"Is everything okay?" I ask. He looks completely surprised by the question. "I mean, the other night, you were a bit stressed out. . . ."

"I'm fine," he says. "Have you told Jack what you heard?"

"Yes," I say. "Honestly he didn't seem that worried. And we met the man who was speaking. I don't suppose he's really a man at all, actually, more of a creature . . . the Earl of October."

He stares at me. "You've met the Earl?"

"What's the problem?"

"Nothing." He looks away. "Just . . . the Earl has a bit of a reputation. He's not so keen on the human interactions. . . ."

"Well, I only saw him for a moment. Then I told Jack he was the one scheming, and now the Earl has summoned Jack to the Royal Court, and I promised I'd be there. . . ." A bunch of kids swarm around us as we pass through the main entrance, breaking my concentration. "So, yes, I said I'd meet him there, but he didn't tell me quite where to go. . . ."

"Seems strange, if he wanted you to be there," Avery says as we get to the history wing.

"Well, he is who he is. . . ."

"I shouldn't tell you."

"But I could swear on a tree never to tell. Or, you

know"—I look around desperately—"on a book, perhaps? Made of the same material, essentially . . ."

"As the Great Oak?" He shakes his head. "You're such a beginner."

I hesitate outside the classroom door while people start heading in. "I need to be there," I say, putting my hand out to stop him. He's rolled up his sleeves and his forearm is covered in minuscule golden freckles. "I'll be careful. . . ."

"What do you think you can do there anyway?"

"I know the truth! I know they're scheming against him. If it all goes wrong for him then I'll be able to explain. . . ."

"It's not a good idea," he says.

"It'll be fine," I insist. "I won't do anything unless I really have to. Besides, don't I have a right to be there? Just as much as you do?"

His nostrils flare as he considers me.

"I can't help you," he says finally, looking down at my hand on his arm with a strange expression. I remove it hurriedly, giving myself a mental slap for being so weird. "I'm sorry, I just can't. You don't know what you're walking into."

With that he strides ahead of me into the classroom, leaving me gaping stupidly after him, completely stung by his response. Maybe it's *not* such a good idea to go to the Royal Court, or to take Mallory for that matter, but I'm not about to let him stop me. What a jerk. We'll just have to do it without him. I can't let Mallory down now. She needs the distraction. It can't be that hard to find, and I need to see it, whatever it might be like. A little shiver of apprehension breaks out on my skin as I settle myself in my usual place, Avery just in front of me, and I keep my coat on for the whole class, just in case it shows.

"I can't believe we're doing this," Mallory whispers as she meets me in the street, her breath puffing out in the cold night air. "I've never done anything like this before!"

"Not sure many people have," I say with a smile as we start walking. I feel really nervous. Avery was so weird about it earlier, it's made me worry. Several times I slow down, wondering whether to tell Mallory we should go back—we still don't know where the Royal Court is meeting, and the Old Druid Wood is enormous—but she's charging on by my side, wrapped up in a heavy coat, a scarf, a hat, and boots with thick socks, happily chatting about whether we're going to see any "real" pixies or elves.

I guess she's thinking of fairy tales.

"I don't think it's going to be quite like that," I hiss as we hike into the sloping field between the school and the forest. The ground is hard with a crisp white frost. I look at my watch: 11:45 p.m.

"It's so cold," Mallory says, slipping as she tries to hurry up the hill. "I guess you don't feel it, but man—"

"Mallory, shh," I whisper, my voice tight as we get closer. The trees cast long shadows in the light of the moon, which is just past full now. "I don't know what this is going to be like. It might be dangerous. Maybe you should wait . . ."

"What, all alone in the dark in this field?" she hisses. "Not likely! I want to meet your dad, anyway. Ja-a-ack Frrrrrossstt," she intones.

I'm not sure I want to see him, though. I'm not sure I'm ready for this Royal Court thing at all. Having seen Jack and the North Wind and the creepy Earl of October, I can hardly imagine what the rest of them will be like. We reach the edge of the trees and I look around furtively, but I can't see much in the darkness.

"How're we going to find it?" Mallory demands, tripping over dry twigs. "It's so dark!"

I've half a mind to turn around right there and pretend none of this is happening at all, but just as I go to say it a tall figure steps between us and grabs us both by our arms, dragging us farther into the tangled undergrowth beneath the trees.

30

"Have you completely lost it?" Avery barks at us, shoving us into the shelter of an enormous ash tree. "Do you know what you're doing, coming here?"

"I said I was coming!" I retort. "And I was hardly going to come alone."

"Besides, surely anyone's allowed into the woods. It's public land, after all," chimes in Mallory. Avery stares at her. She stares back.

"It's not safe," he says, his eyes roaming, searching the woodland around us. "This isn't some cozy fairy land! Humans aren't allowed at the Royal Court. You might get away with it," he says looking at me. "But I'm not sure it's even possible for Mallory to get there. And if you're here for Jack it's about the worst thing you could do, to bring her with you. . . ."

"Well, we're here now," I say, folding my arms. "And I'm guessing you're not king of the wood, so you've no choice in it. You should go. We'll make our own way. You didn't want to be seen with me, remember?"

He draws me to one side. "Seriously, Owl, stop this. It's not safe for either of you, especially not for Mallory." He looks me up and down, his eyes softening. "Even you won't be able to fight them all off, if they discover you."

"Would they really attack us?"

"I don't know," he says, shifting his feet, his eyes constantly on the lookout. "I don't know what will happen. I just know some of them won't like it. And, as I say, she might not even get through."

"Get through where?"

"There's a barrier. A spell, I suppose. It stops humans from seeing what they're not supposed to see."

"So she'll be there, but she won't see anything?"

"I don't know!" he hisses, his shoulders tense. "I don't know what will happen. Are you really willing to risk it?"

The branches of the trees rustle around us and there's a low scurrying noise, things stirring in the undergrowth. Avery looks back to the deep darkness of the wood.

"The trees are waking," he whispers. "Go *home*, Owl. There's nothing for you here." His eyes blaze and the trees around us lower their branches with a shuffle and a cascade of leaves, snapping upright once more when he waves his hand at them with a frustrated huff. "Please," he says. "This isn't a place for humans—just go." And with that he's off, darting through the trees as if he's been doing it all his life. He probably has, I think with a shudder as I turn back to Mallory.

"Wow. Was that, with the trees . . . Did he do that? Did they *bow* to him, Owl? Is this place *really* full of strange creatures?" she asks, her voice hushed.

"I did try to tell you," I whisper, a knot forming in my stomach as I look around us.

The trees seem closer together now. They're so tall they could be endless. The light is dim already and farther in, darkness clings to every limb.

We tread through thick undergrowth in the direction Avery went, trying to steer clear of the trees. It gets darker as we go, and the night sounds grow louder: the movement of unseen creatures, the creak of the trees in the wind. I forge through, Mallory following, her hand on my jacket. My eyes are quick to adapt to the darkness, every sense on alert, but Mallory blunders behind me, her breath quick and hard.

"Owl!" she hisses suddenly, as a whisper of wind breaks over my skin.

"Mall?" I turn as she breaks away from me, blinking and searching out with her hands.

"Where are you?"

"Right here!"

"I can't see you," she says, panic edging her voice. I take a step toward her, feel that same whisper against my skin. "There you are! It's so dark. . . ." Mallory breathes.

"I don't think it's that, Mallory," I say, searching for a sign of the barrier. It's invisible, whatever it is. "It's a spell, meant to hide the Royal Court from humans. Can you get through?"

I step back through the barrier and pull her with me, but her hands are ripped from mine as she bounces back.

"Oh, my goodness," I whisper, helping her up. "Mallory, it's not going to let you through!"

"So . . . I'll wait here for you then. You go on." She looks very pale as she says it, though her jaw is set with determination.

"I can't do that, Mall!"

"Yes, you can," she says, her voice stronger. "I've got a flashlight, and my personal alarm, and a bit of chocolate. . . ."

"I'm not sure . . ."

"Seriously, Owl, go. This is important. I'll be fine. I'll just sit in this pile of leaves here"—she shuffles them together and plonks herself down in the middle—"and eat my chocolate."

I stand for a few minutes watching her, making sure

she's okay, and when I can see she's absorbed in a game on her phone I force myself to go on through the barrier. The creaking of trees is louder on the other side, and there's a charge in the air, as if the whole place is alive with magic. By the time I come out into a small clearing, the telltale tingling of my skin has started. I look down at my hands to see they're covered in frost that glitters beneath the clear moonlight.

And then I look up.

And any doubt I might have had about everything that's happened disappears, blown to pieces by the scene unfolding before me.

31

FABLES & EARTH SPIRITS

The Lady of the Lake

Deep down in the murk of underwater, the girl thought that she was drowning. She thought that she had taken a wrong turn somehow in the incantation and her adventures in the magical lands of the fay folk were over. Her chest burned as she breathed in water, and she fought to push herself up to the surface, but she fought in vain. Her feet were tangled in the rough, grasping roots that twisted through the riverbed.

"No, child, forget your struggles," came a voice, and it seemed that it rang within her head, and there was a bright light and she thought that surely this was the end. Then pale hands clutched her shoulders and pulled her forward through the water until, with a kiss that broke

upon her face, the underbelly of the lake revealed itself to her: a vast bubble of air within the water, and within that bubble such a place that for an instant she wondered if she had perished after all, and this was heaven.

She stood in a puddle of water, breathing hard and so very aware of her sorry, bedraggled state, and she could find no words to explain herself, though the question was in the eyes of all the assembly before her. They were fairies and water-sprites, and other, taller figures that she could not name, with gills upon their slender necks. Their glittering skin was bright beneath the chandeliers that dangled from the roof of the cavernous hall. Quartz had made this place, and a million points of pink light shone out from every corner.

"Well, child, and what mischief have you found yourself in this time?" came the voice once more. "Come forward to me, I would see your face . . ."

The otherworldly figures parted to reveal a pale, marble throne, upon which sat a pale lady more beautiful than words could ever tell. The girl forgot that she had nearly drowned, forgot her dripping hair, her chilled skin, for the lady was heat and light and peace.

"I have heard of you," she said with a gentle smile. "You are our traveler, our human interloper. You shall find trouble, sooner or later, if you carry on with your little spell. I wonder how you came by it. . . ."

The lady looked at her straight in the eye and in that moment it was as if she read the whole of her being.

"It does not offend me to have you here," she said, almost as if surprised by that. She waved an elegant hand at the crowd and it dissipated. "Will you write of your adventures, traveler?" she asked, when they were alone.

The girl could only stare. She could no more think of writing at that moment than she could have wielded a fish to fight a sword.

"I think perhaps you should," the lady said, her silver eyes bright with the thought. "Write it, and hide it well, and we shall see if your adventures one day might have a purpose. They say all things have meaning. . . ." She stepped forward, over the pale shell floor, and then was in front of the girl. She stooped, and breathed upon her. "Now," she said. "Begone, and if you should continue with your travels take heed of my warning. Not all will welcome you."

32

Mom's read those legends all my life—about the figures who watch over nature, about the beauty and the danger of the elements—but they were bedtime stories, and they never frightened me. Those fairy-tale characters were magical, vivid beings who lived in another world, a world of books and movies and imagination. They weren't living, real creatures.

Except they were, and they're right before me now. The trees have opened out into a clearing that dips down to a lake I've never seen here before. It's like the whole place has been transported from Mom's old storybook. The water is still, shining silver beneath the moon, and all around it, between pale globe lights that rise out of the moss-covered ground, are strange, almost human figures that my mind is fighting to accept.

The Earl of October sits on a great stone bench overlooking the lake, his long knotted limbs all awkward angles. Next to him sits a curvy woman in a hooded robe, her green eyes glinting like metal as she looks around the gathering. Beside her is an old man, thick-set and dark skinned, his iron-gray hair in matted strands standing up around his head. On the other side of the Earl is a tiny woman, perhaps a sprite, her knees drawn up to her chest, and a man, hardly bigger. He turns to talk to her and I notice with a shudder that his teeth are mirror bright and sharp as knives.

Gathered around the edge of the lake are dozens of other figures. Most of them are sprites like the tiny figures on the bench, their skin sparkling in the light in shades of green and tawny brown. There are more of the shadowy goblins and other, pale, winged creatures, perhaps fairies, in the branches of the trees, their faces sharp, bright hair standing out around their heads in wild ringlets. They're beautiful and somehow terrible, too. The air rings with a cold steel as they move from one tree to another with a blur of silver wings. The trees themselves are no more comforting, standing tall and slender all around the court, moving in apparent conversation with each other, roots twisting beneath the earth, branches sweeping low in strange, almost human gestures. Deep in the undergrowth other creatures stir: a hedgehog, and what I think might be a weasel, its eyes gleaming in the darkness.

As I watch, spellbound, a giant white owl swoops down over my head toward the clearing, landing on the lake in ghostly grace, its talons outspread, and then a pale woman with long, silver hair rises through the water, the owl perched on one narrow wrist. The Lady of the Lake, it must be. She stares around the clearing, and there's a sudden stillness. Many of the figures lower their heads at her arrival, though I notice the Earl doesn't, and neither does the woman sitting next to him.

"We are met," she says, her voice carrying easily through the clearing. "All but the one summoned, I see. . . ."

"He'll be here," the Earl says, his tone clipped. "He wouldn't miss the chance to be the center of attention. Avery!"

My breath gets stuck in my throat as Avery steps forward out of the gloom at the far end of the lake. His head is lowered, his shoulders round, as if he's trying to disappear into the earth itself.

"Yes?"

"My son has been acting on our behalf in the human world," says the Earl to the gathered crowd. "So, what have you for us?" His cold eyes flick up and down Avery dispassionately and Avery shifts his feet, keeping his eyes on the ground.

He's the Earl's *son*.

My heart thumps and a sheen of frost spreads instantly over my limbs. It won't compute. He must have known, when we spied on them. That was why he stumbled and ran away, he didn't want me to hear what they were saying. And then later, when I told him I'd met the Earl . . . he said nothing! Nothing except that the Earl wasn't a fan of humankind.

"I . . ."

"Come on, speak up!" shouts someone from the edge of the lake. "What have you learned from your time at the human school?"

A smattering of laughter bursts out around the clearing, though the Lady in the Lake does not smile, her eyes hard on the Earl before shifting to Avery.

"Tell us what you have found," she says gently. "We must know, if we are to make decisions."

Avery trains his eyes on the Lady, and when he speaks his voice is clear.

"She is modestly talented. She has some of his traits. She exhibits some signs of them in public, though not enough that it has been noticed. She is unusual. . . ."

I can barely stand still, I'm so furious. He lied to me. Over and over, he pretended to be interested, to be my friend. He poured all that doubt on my stories of spies and it turns out he was the biggest spy of them all! All this time he's just been getting information, working for his father. This cannot be happening. I cannot have been *this* much of an idiot.

No wonder he didn't want me to be here.

"Unusual?" barks the Earl. "I should think so, being who she is! She can hardly be a standard human, can she? And yet she does not belong with us, either."

Avery flinches, looking down at the ground again.

"Does her power grow? Can she control it?" the Lady asks.

"I don't know," he says. "There is no . . . there is no . . ." He runs his hand through his hair, clears his throat. "She is powerful, a bit chaotic. But there is no reason to think she would be a danger, either here or there."

"That is not for you to judge," the Earl says in a harsh voice, gesturing for Avery to return to the shadows.

"Thank you, Avery," says the Lady. "We must discuss this carefully, my dear Earl. We cannot disappear a human easily."

Disappear a human? An icy shudder rolls over me, but I plant my feet more firmly into the cold ground, determined to hear this out. Determined to help Jack, if I can. At least *he* hasn't lied to me.

"Of course there will be careful discussion, my Lady," the Earl says. "As leader of this cycle I shall endeavor to ensure every law of this Royal Fay Court of Mother

Earth is upheld, and that every obligation is satisfied."

The Lady turns slightly from him, her expression unreadable. I try to breathe normally, increasingly aware of how vulnerable I am here, how easy it would be for someone to spot me in the shadow of the trees. I shift my weight to ease the growing numbness in my feet, and my elbow grazes the outermost branch of a huge oak tree behind me.

The owl lifts its head and looks directly into my eyes.

My heart swells as it studies me, and I find myself taking a step toward the lake as the tree behind me shifts into me. I spin, my heart hammering in my chest, to see the roots and branches of the oak gathering together with impossible speed, forming a great oaken giant of a man.

"Green Man!" the Lady calls. "I hear you stirring. Come, join us!"

"There are more interesting creatures than me with us today," the strange tree figure rumbles behind me, reaching out and grasping me at the waist between his thickened, twisted fingers. "I have a stray here. What creature is this?"

I shriek and try to escape as he steps forward with me, holding me at arm's length as if I smell bad. A gasp rolls through the crowd gathered below and I notice a sparkle in the Earl's eyes. He looks delighted, and I realize that somehow my being here has only made things better for him. I fight harder to get away from the Green Man as we near the lake. People part to make way for the lumbering tree figure, and as I kick against him the owl rises from the Lady's wrist, coming toward me on silent, powerful wings. It circles the Green Man, getting closer and closer until he's forced to stop.

"What is it?" he grumbles. "Do you not like my prisoner?" He looks at me with his hollow eyes, and I cannot make out the expression in them at all. "She does not look like a terrible danger to me."

The owl flaps harder, blowing my hair back from my face. She looks at me and I am caught there, in the blink of her eye, in a moment so vast, so full of possibility, that I can hardly breathe.

And then the Green Man staggers back, and the spell is broken.

"By!" he roars. "Night creature, here, you may have her!" He thrusts me onto the ground and the owl stops her silent attack, gliding back to the Lady, who has been watching it all with what just might be humor on her narrow face.

"So," she says, looking me up and down as I hurry to my feet, feeling exposed and a bit horrified at having been hurled around by a tree. "You must be the daughter of Jack Frost."

"I am," I say, my voice wobbling, but carrying quite nicely, given the circumstances.

"And what is your given name?"

I glance at the owl, who blinks her enormous yellow eyes at me.

Courage, Owl.

"I'm called Owl," I say.

There's a commotion in the crowd. I back away, wondering if I can just run, but the Earl stands, raising his long arms. The woman next to him doesn't move a muscle, but her eyes glint as she watches me.

"Enough!" shouts the Earl, clapping his hands together, a flurry of autumn leaves cascading from the trees. "This is the Royal Court! There shall be order here. Girl." He turns to me, face tight with rage. "Do you dare to stand there and lie to us all?"

"I'm not lying!" I retort, flinching as he claps his gnarled hands together.

"Avery!"

"Yes, Father?" Avery looks more stooped than even before as he steps forward.

"You knew of this name?"

"Yes, Father."

"And you did not tell us?"

"I did not see the significance," mumbles Avery, his face flushed.

"She is named after our herald!" the Earl roars. "She is connected to it!"

"The owl is our friend, dear Earl," says the Lady smoothly. "She means us no harm. And if she is connected to the girl, what does that matter? We were not about to harm her, were we?"

"She is a danger," says the woman next to the Earl in a smooth, melodic voice that seems familiar, staring at me. "Avery has told us she is chaotic. And above all else she is clear evidence that Jack has forgotten his place in the world. . . ."

"Did you speak of me?" says a voice behind me. Jack steps forward, as if he's been here all along. *Perhaps he has*, I think, looking at the pinched expression on his face. Though he's dwarfed in height by some of the others here, his presence is far greater, the air around him rings cold and bright with his power. "Shall we begin, old friend? This is no child of mine. It is not possible. Her only crime is delusion. And her connection to the bird may well explain her peculiarities. . . ." My heart twists painfully in my chest: he's so harsh. There's no doubt, no question in his voice. He dismisses me as though I truly am nothing to him, even after the time we've spent together.

"The connection to the 'bird' is not the issue here," says the Lady in an acid tone. "If anything it is a good thing—perhaps she is wiser than some of us. Jack, you are mistaken. *Look* at the girl. She is more clearly yours than Avery is *his* father's. . . ."

The crowd of figures around the lake begins to talk loudly. Some of them are truly outraged at my presence, and most seem at least a little flustered. Avery lifts his head, just slightly, though he won't look in my direction.

If he did I might decide to try out my laser ice eyes. I mean, I *might* have them. They would be useful in this situation.

I can't believe he's been spying on me.

I can't believe how much it hurts.

"Silence!" shouts the Earl after a moment, standing to full height, his skin mottled with rage. "We all know of my previous indiscretion. I was punished for it! Two long years of solitude—I paid my debt. And Avery has served us well over the years." He refuses to look at his son. Instead his dark, glinting eyes are focused on me and my father. "Besides, I am not one of the elementals, though autumn is my charge. It is *forbidden* for them to consort with humans in any way! This is a most heinous crime, and one that I demand is met with like punishment!"

There's a swell of agreement in the crowd. Jack and I stand in the midst of it now, and he's like a storm beside me, the very air freezing around us.

"What does that mean?" the Lady asks in a calm voice. "What would you do?"

"He must be banished!"

"It is his season, and he is Jack Frost! We cannot banish him just as winter begins."

A crafty look comes over the Earl's face, though he is quick to assume a neutral expression, one of humility, almost.

"It is not an easy decision," he says. "We all know of Jack's power, of the importance of his job, but he has grown arrogant over the years. He does not work to serve Mother Earth—he does it for his own pleasure and pride. Evenings spent dancing on ice, splintering windows just because he can. These things cannot go unpunished forever!"

"What do you charge me with?" Jack asks in a leaden voice. "With being myself? It is not a crime. I am not a servant to mankind, or to order. I am not some fussing minor creature, bent on nothing more than gaining power over my peers. What power I have is mine, given to me by Mother Earth herself. I am who I am, what I am. Winter's edge is pitiless as it makes its way across the world—without it, all would perish."

"No matter what else is said," the woman next to the Earl puts in as she lowers her hood, palest pink hair falling to her waist, "you have broken one of the fundamental laws of this Royal Court, Jack. You have consorted with humanity. You have created a creature half human and half of yourself." She shoots me a venomous look and I feel a shock of recognition. That pink hair, that voice . . . She's the Queen of May, the one we overheard talking with the Earl that day. She's behind this, and she's not about to let it go now. "It cannot go unmarked," she continues. "Chaos would ensue. If the North Wind could spawn children, if the Morning Star had a flock of his own, the world would be changed forever."

There are murmurs of assent. I close my eyes and pinch myself, but the sense of magic is still thick in the air, and my father beside me is a physical manifestation of the most glacial rage there has ever been.

"I did no such thing!" he protests.

"Why, Jack?" asks the Lady. "Why do you persist in this lie? Have you not seen it for yourself? Look upon her! Have you ever seen such a creature?"

He turns his eyes to me. My heart thuds as he looks me up and down, his silver eyes cool and assessing. I try to stay calm, try not to care one way or another, but there is no recognition there, not a sign that he cares for me at all. It wells up inside me and breaks, tears sliding down my cheeks to land as tiny ice crystals at my feet.

"It isn't possible!" he bursts out, thin-lipped and pale with outrage, looking back at the Lady. "I was made for one thing only." His voice grows bitter. "I was made to herald winter, to travel the world alone, spreading the message that it was on its way. I have no mortality! I cannot create life!"

The Lady breaks in and I think she's saying something about change, but Jack isn't listening—he's staring at me again, his eyes glittering, his hair thick with ice, and I don't hear her either. I'm too busy wondering if he's changing his mind.

"A vote, I think," breaks in the Earl. "Let us vote. Whether or not Jack will admit fathering this creature is irrelevant. He is not a character to be trusted either way and that much he has proven well over the centuries. We can all see the truth here. Raise your hand if you consider him guilty of this crime!"

Jack says nothing. He folds his arms and looks up at the sky as if he couldn't care less.

"But wait!" My breath unleashes with a flurry of ice and everything stops, everything is still around me. I didn't mean to speak, and yet here it is. My blood races as I realize this is the moment. This is the moment I could change things. A thousand inhuman eyes are all fixed on me, most of them unfriendly. I focus on the Lady. "They have plotted against him, they've been planning this all along!"

"How dare you?" shouts the Earl, standing to his full height, his fists clenched at his sides. He takes a great thumping step toward me, his narrow, mottled face contorted with rage. "How dare you interrupt the proceeds of this Royal Court, you—"

"My dear Earl!" chides the Lady. "She is a child. She is *Jack's* child, as you have charged her."

"The children of humans have no voice in the Royal Court," says the Queen, her voice calm despite a sudden blaze of color through her cheeks. Her pink hair whips out around her face. "If she must be here, then she must be silent."

"But this is what you wanted!" I shout, fear turning into adrenaline, spiking through my veins, running icy fingers through my hair. "You and—"

"Stop this!" demands the Earl in a cracking voice. He takes a deep breath and steps back to the bench, lowering himself with a creak and folding his arms. "Enough. I have charged the Royal Court with Jack's fate. We cannot let this creature stand in the way of that."

"Nor will we," says the Lady, her voice suddenly weary. "Let us proceed. Sit, child. He is right. You have no sway here."

Jack puts his hand on my arm, but I refuse to look at him. He didn't fight at all. He just stood there and let them shut me up. I risk a look at Avery, who cannot help but meet my eye. He bites his lip and shrugs as hands shoot up into the air from all directions: sprites, fairies, even some of the trees thrusting forward pale, twisted branches—far, far too many to be outvoted.

Jack is going to be banished, and there's nothing I can do about it.

Look what you did! I howl at Avery in my mind, blinking back tears.

He lowers his head.

"It is done," the Earl says with a sigh of relief. The Queen is silent beside him, but the look on her face is of pure delight.

"You cannot banish me!" Jack roars, stalking forward, down the bank to the lake. "My Lady! You cannot let this happen!" The water begins to freeze as he storms toward it and the Lady takes a step back.

"Jack," she says. "You are hiding from yourself. If you cannot see the truth in the charges, how may I help you? How may you be defended? The Earl is in his power still, and the vote has been cast. You have left your protest too late."

"No!" he shouts. "This is my time! You cannot cast me out now. Are you so blind? Do you not see how important my work is?"

"We will find a way around it," the Lady says, her voice growing tight, as ice rolls out like smoke around her. "Accept this, Jack, and return to your domain. It will not be forever!"

“I will not!” he says, fixing his eyes on the Earl. He takes another step forward, onto the frozen lake, as storm clouds swirl overhead and tiny daggers of hail begin to fall. The owl takes flight and the Lady brings her hands down hard onto the ice, splintering it into great chunks that fly up into the air around Jack, who flounders in suddenly turbulent waters.

“I have a fond regard for thee,” the Lady says to him in a low voice that makes the air shudder. “But you are not in power when you step into my territory. You have been charged, and found guilty. Now, GO!” She brings her arms together and the waters rage around him until he is forced to drag himself out, pale and bedraggled.

I race toward him, straining to see through hail and snow, my shoulders hunched against it, but he glances at me and puts out a restraining hand. “Not now,” he says, his voice tense. “I must go where I am bid.” He gives me a fleeting whisper of a smile. “Fly while I am gone, little Owl. Remember all I have shown you and have no mercy, for the world is a cruel place and that is necessary. Life cannot flourish without a fight.”

“Where’s *your* fight?” I ask, ignoring the rest of the Royal Court, ice forming with every step I take. My skin glitters in the murky moonlight, and my heart is sinking, for I found him and now I’ll lose him, and still he hasn’t acknowledged me, even after all this. He will just leave me here with all these strangers who call me "creature" as if I am something cursed and wrong. "Won't you fight to stay, to do your work? For me?"

He moves close, his voice low. The ground is white around us, even as the hail dies away. Fingers of frost stretch from my feet to his, meeting and blooming in the middle, spreading out across the grass to meet the restless roots of nearby trees.

"I cannot stay. They will not allow me. If I fight for you then we are both lost. You cannot be mine. It is not possible!"

"But you *remembered* her, when I talked to you before. You remembered the dark-haired woman who is my mother!"

"She was a *dream*, sent to fill one lonely day of many, many millions," he says, shaking his head, not meeting my eye. "All creatures may have their dreams, even if they have nothing else." He turns from me and strides into the darkness. "Follow your own dreams, little Owl. . . ."

"Isolde!" I call out after him, through a mist of last hopes. "Her name is Isolde!"

He hesitates then. But he does not turn. The eyes of all the Royal Court are on him as he pauses for just a moment. Then he breaks out into a run, and in another moment he is gone.

33

They're all looking at me, now. I'm trying not to notice but I can feel dozens of eyes on me, watching every move. I raise my head eventually and focus on the Lady of the Lake. I will not look at the Earl, though I can't help but notice how proudly he sits on the stone bench, now that he has won. The Queen beside him is even more full of it. She seems to glow with satisfaction.

"What shall we do with thee, child?" the Lady asks, her voice gentle.

"She is no child to be pitied and coddled," the Earl says impatiently. "She is the daughter of mischief and mayhem. She is capable of things that make her most dangerous."

"And yet she is a child," the Lady replies. "I do not know that there is an easy decision here. What do you want to do, Owl?"

What *do* I want to do? I want to go after my father and drag him back. I want him to fight for me. I want to go back to school and forget any of this ever happened. I know I don't want to be here anymore, with Avery stealing guilty glances at me.

"I want to go home."

"And yet it isn't so simple." She shakes her head. "You cannot just go about your own people as you did before. . . ."

"Impossible for her to remain here!" the Earl exclaims, standing.

"Will you find her too challenging?" the Lady demands. "Are you so weak in your own power that you will not allow an innocent child to remain with us?"

"How about a challenge?" asks the Queen in her soft, melodic voice, soothing the Earl with a hand on his arm. "We should give the girl a choice." She looks at me, and for a split second her full mouth twists with a hatred that makes my spine curl. "My dear," she says, covering it with a smile that is somehow even more chilling. "You may, of course, stay here. Your friend Avery has known the comfort of the Royal Court for most of his life. Why shouldn't you too know the magic of our existence? He has told you stories already, I expect, of our family. We are many and varied. We live by the sun and the moon and are masters of all that surrounds us here. Life, death, every decision made for the common good. Games and trials, enough to turn your head so that you may never think of home again. . . ." She pauses for a moment and looks up at the fairies, who are spellbound by her words. "Or . . . if that doesn't suit you . . ." She turns back to me, her eyes suddenly gleaming. "Go back out into your world and do your father's work for him! Show us that you can control your power, that even out there you are loyal to us and a part of the work we do."

"But . . ." Avery steps forward, flinching as his father looks at him. "But she cannot!"

"Why not?" the Queen demands with another hideous smile. "She is Jack's daughter. She has already shown us she has his skills. You said as much yourself, dear Avery. If she doesn't want to turn away from humanity, she may do this thing for us all, for humanity itself—may she not?"

"It would *change* her. She is already—" Avery begins.

"Enough!" the Earl spits. "Avery, you forget yourself! This is Royal Court *business*! Get out of my sight. I will deal with you later!"

Avery stands against him for just a moment, moonlight breaking through the clouds and casting him in silver, his jaw working, then he steps back into the darkness.

"What do you say, Owl?" the Lady asks, looking at me. Her gray eyes are steady, but the water around her bubbles and surges, as though she's trying to hide her anger. Is she on my side? Will she let them do this to me? What choice is it really? I can't stay here, they can all see that much. The very ground seems to writhe beneath me. "It is not what you will have expected, but the Queen is right. You are a part of this world now. If you are to leave it, you will still have to live as one of us and prove that you can be true to this Royal Court. Your father's work will suit you. . . ." Her voice trails off and she sighs. "It is up to you, Owl. None can make you do it."

"I'll do it," I hear myself saying as if from very far away. "I can do it." I have a quick, impulsive thought. "If I do it well, will you let him come back?"

"You are in no position to strike bargains," sneers the Earl.

"We'll see," says the Lady. "If you can prove yourself an asset to us, we may be able to reconsider things . . . but do not count on it, Owl. If you choose it, you choose it for yourself. Not in hope for others."

I nod, my head spinning. Suddenly it feels as though all my blood has frozen in my veins, as if I cannot move, cannot speak. I look around me and everything is black and white, light and shade. Globe-like eyes peer at me from all sides and I want nothing more than to run.

"Avery," the Lady says, her voice faint. "See that she gets home safely."

"Yes, go," rumbles the Earl. "Continue at the human school and report back to us regularly. Take her now and be sure she does not act, does not *move*, without your knowledge. It is on your head, boy. If you want to earn a place in this Royal Court, perhaps here is your chance. . . ."

"Yes, Father." Avery dips his head and I hate him for it. More than anything else, I hate the way he stoops and bends before his cruel father, who seems to see him as nothing more than a tool for his own ambitions.

I stumble up the bank back toward the ranks of trees, Avery just behind me, and the Green Man stoops to sweep me up onto even ground.

"Careful how you go, little Owl," he says in a creaking whisper. "We will be wishing you success." I turn to see that there is sympathy in the eyes of some of the Royal Court. "But do not bring your human friend here again. I have kept her safe this time, but she does not belong. . . ."

The owl swoops down to me as I head into the darkness and lands on my shoulder. "Your way. Your way, little Owl," she says in her soft hoot of a voice. "Do it your way . . ." And then she's off, and Avery catches up with me, and I have to concentrate just to keep my breathing level, my footsteps sure.

❄❄❄

"What did you do with Mallory?" he asks as we skirt through the trees. He steps through undergrowth with no sound at all, while I am an elephant careening through, my feet picking fights with all the roots. I cannot find my voice to answer him. I'm not sure what I'd say if I could. His presence cuts into me, so that I have to charge on faster, faster, just to get away from the sickening smell of woodsmoke that I always thought I liked. I'm almost running by the time I feel the kiss of the barrier against my skin, and there, in the shadows, her face blue lit by the screen of her phone, is Mallory.

"Mall!" I whisper, hurrying to her, a sudden lump in my throat.

"Owl! But are you not going to go to the Royal Court? Did he stop you?" She scrambles up and looks askance at Avery, which I could hug her for.

"It's all over," I whisper. "Maybe time's different in there. It feels like I've been gone for ages. I'm so glad you're safe."

She frowns and steps forward, giving me a quick, tight hug.

"Are you okay?" she asks in a low voice, pulling me away from Avery, who shifts his feet and gazes at the ground. He looks utterly miserable but he's still here, doing as his father bid, and as we move on toward the edge of the woodland he dogs our steps.

I don't think I've ever felt so betrayed by another person. I trusted him with everything. He knew who I really was before *I* did. I thought we were the same, but I hardly knew him at all. Mallory keeps her eyes on me as we tread over dark, twisted roots, arm in arm. I'm so glad she's here, I feel like if she weren't I'd just be in a heap by the trees. She holds tight to me, even though my skin is cold with ice, and when she speaks her voice is soft.

"Tell me, what happened?"

"He got banished, for being my father! Even though he was determined he wasn't. They could all see it, more easily than he could."

"He's gone?"

"Yup."

"Oh, Owl."

"And now Avery will be 'watching over me' while I try to do what Jack normally does. He spied on me, Mallory, for his father. . . ." I tell her in a halting voice about the Earl and the Queen, and the bargain I've struck, and the silence in the woodland gets thicker and darker, and always, always, Avery's light steps follow ours.

"But how is that going to work?" Mallory demands after she's listened. "You're a girl, Owl. You're not Jack Frost!"

"But I'm not a normal girl either."

"Nobody's normal," she says. "You're just *extra*, that's all."

I smile at her determined tone, but I still feel small and tight with foreboding. How *can* I take over from him? Does he travel the world, putting the frost on everything? It's always winter somewhere. How am I going to do all that?

Avery steps forward as we emerge into the park. The moon is a small bright disk in the sky now, throwing silver outlines over everything. Skeletal trees loom over the terraced houses and the shadows are deeper than they seemed before. A breeze spins up and whips over my face and I think it might be Avery's work and so I hate that it's welcome, almost soothing, against my skin.

"They're looking for a gesture," he says, his eyes on the cluttered suburban horizon. "Jack's not responsible for winter, or even for all of the frost and ice. He's the one who hangs icicles, puts fern patterns on windows . . . warns people across the world that winter is on its way and reminds them that it's beautiful, even while it's treacherous."

"How will I get to all those places?" I demand, refusing to look at him.

Avery shakes his head. "You can't. They won't expect you to. The Queen knows it as well as anyone. Just do the bare minimum, any more than that is dangerous for you."

"Dangerous?" asks Mallory.

"The more you do, the more you could lose yourself to the magic. It's tricky for a half human, Owl, I told you."

"So that's the Queen's plan? To ruin me by making me do Jack's work?"

"Probably," he whispers.

"And you knew, didn't you? You knew what they were plotting. You *helped them*! All this time . . . you were spying on me! Reporting back to your *father*!"

He flinches. "I did try to—"

"What is his problem anyway?" I interrupt. "What does he even get out of this?"

"He craves power," Avery says. "And he has a grudge against Jack."

"A grudge?" My voice sounds unstable now, even to me. "All of this over a grudge?"

"They're powerful things, grudges, when you live forever. . . ."

"What is it? What did Jack do?"

"I don't know," Avery replies. "My . . . The Earl would never say. Something happened, a long time ago. I'm sorry, Owl, let me—"

"No," I say through my clenched teeth. "Don't pretend like you care now. Just go!" My voice becomes a howl and frost zips toward him over the grass.

He steps back, suddenly clumsy. "You need to let me help you!"

"I *thought* that was what you were doing before! I'll never trust you again, Avery!"

I grab Mallory and we charge off toward the dark street, and to her credit she doesn't complain, though I'm breathing in flurries of ice and my hand must be freezing her arm.

"We'll work it out," she says as we part. "I promise, Owl. I'll help. We'll sort it." She gives me a hug and I try to return it, but I feel like something has shifted. Like something on the inside is frozen solid, so that I can't. I can't even hug my best friend properly.

The feeling stays with me all the way home, and I'm dimly aware that it's lucky Mom hasn't woken while I was out, but I don't really care. I'm back in my room, and even here everything feels different. I'm surrounded by all my pictures of owls, and I've already managed to freeze the entire room, so it almost feels like I'm back in that clearing once more, only all the fay—the sprites and fairies and creepy goblins—are now the owls, all of them watching me, demanding in hoarse whispers that I "open my eyes" and "see the truth" in it all.

"What do you mean?" I demand, looking from one to

the next as they blink their crazy eyes and shuffle their charcoal feathers. "Tell me!"

They say nothing more. They just watch as the ice spreads to the ceiling in great spears that sparkle in the dim light of my bedside lamp. I sit, exhausted, and the room seems to darken and I am lost, lost, lost in the middle, marooned on my frozen bed.

He rejected me.

In front of the whole Royal Court, he refused to acknowledge that he was my father. Even though they could all see it.

Hadn't I expected that? Hadn't I known he would never really be a father? I look in the mirror and see how small I am, and I realize that it doesn't matter. It doesn't matter that I already knew it, it doesn't matter *what* he is—he is my father, and he would rather be banished from this world than to accept it. Ice slides down my cheeks and I don't wipe it away—I close my eyes and let it fall.

"Little Owl," says the wooden owl on the bedpost with a clatter and snap of its wooden beak. "Hush, now. Not so much is different. Not so much that you cannot handle it."

I reach up and stroke the wood, shocked to find it warm, and too tired and heart sore to question it any longer.

"You *are* real."

"As real as you. As real as this room." The owl looks around, wooden feathers shuffling with a sound like dominoes falling. "Sleep, little Owl. None can get to you here. . . ."

34

FABLES & EARTH SPIRITS

The Green Man

It was something that came to her that she could never quite explain. Perhaps it was a dream, perhaps some fay magic was on the loose and found her quite by accident. However it had transpired, there it was, the words were in her head, and though she tried to let them rest there, they were not content. They demanded, that night, by the light of the candle, to be spoken out loud.

She knew not what she did. Her breath grew heavy, her very mind seemed to fracture, mirror-like shards that splintered silver in the darkness, and then she was out in a new world, where the stars shone brighter and the earth smelled richer and all that was there was the most enormous, ancient oak tree, tangled branches filling the horizon.

"By, and what do we have here?" came a great, rumbling voice. She fell to her knees and gaped as the tree turned, with a ground-shaking twist of root and limb, and formed the body of a most enormous oaken giant with a beaming, delighted expression upon his creviced face. "What creature are you, child, to chance upon an old man in his rest? Have you come to play?"

She shook her head, dumbfounded, and he chuckled, lowering his head, the branches that made his hair reaching down to tickle at her feet. She squirmed, and shuffled away from him, and he grew quite still, until she began to be afraid of him.

"You are not of the fay at all," he said in wonderment, standing tall once more and casting out all light. "How then do you appear thus? Do you seek trouble?"

"No!" she managed. "I am only—only lost. Where is this place?"

"You wander and have found the fay world quite by accident? How extraordinary." He thought for a moment and then reached out to her with a massive, gnarled hand. "Come, that I may keep you warm, and I shall tell you of our hidden world, for you are here now, and there are things you should know."

She ventured forth and climbed into his hand, entranced by his otherness and too befuddled to refuse. And he told her countless tales of sprites and fairies, strange woodland creatures and even stranger water-dwellers, of adventure, and danger, and she thought she dreamed as she sat and listened to the gentle rumble of his voice and the wind through his leaves, but she had never had a sweeter dream, not for all that she found in future times that it was no dream at all.

35

"You look tired, Owl," Mom says in the morning. "Are you feeling okay?" She comes up and puts a hand on my forehead.

"Ach, get off," I mumble, moving away from her, pretending not to see the frown on her face. I'm stiff with tiredness, trying not to let last night replay in my mind as it did throughout my dreams. When I woke, the room looked normal again, the sun casting rays of white light through the gap in the curtains onto piles of books and dusty shelves, and I looked at all my owls and wondered if I'd dreamed that bit, but the wooden owl winked at me when I stared at her, so I know it was real.

"You feel a bit cold," Mom says, putting the kettle on. "Why don't you put a sweater on?"

"Why don't *you* put a sweater on?" I retort absently.

She gives me a look. "I *have* a sweater on," she says, gesturing at the fuchsia pink mohair thing I remember her buying at a yard sale. "I'm talking about you."

"Well, I'm the daughter of Jack Frost so I don't feel the cold particularly, thank you," I say, sitting at the table, splaying my legs out and leaning my head back against the wall.

Mom shakes her head.

"Oatmeal?"

"Yes, please."

"What are you thinking?" she asks, putting a mug of tea in front of me.

"About how we've always lived here, and nothing really changes. . . ."

"Is that a good thing?"

"I s'pose so," I say, sitting up and putting my hands around the mug. A little mist of condensation forms on the china.

"Lots of things change," she says, turning to the oatmeal. "You change all the time. Sometimes it's nice to have something familiar to return to, no?"

"I guess so," I say again, blowing onto the hot tea, instantly cooling it.

"So . . . about Jack," she says after a moment, her voice hesitant. "Have you thought any more about trying to find him?"

The tea freezes in the mug.

"Um. No. I mean, I've been a bit distracted, what with Mallory's parents, and then Avery . . ."

"The boy," she says, taking bowls from the cupboard. "You like him?"

"No!"

She smiles broadly, coming to the table.

"How wonderful!" she exclaims. She doesn't notice the frozen tea and I concentrate very hard on making sure the oatmeal doesn't go the same way. She watches me while I eat, as if she's trying to work out what's going on in my head. I hope she can't. I'm losing track of all the lies I've told her. What if I were to tell her everything now? I play out the conversation in my mind, ending with how Jack's been exiled and I'm going to be doing his work. I'm honestly not sure what she'd make of it all. She can be quite surprising sometimes, but she'd definitely be hurt by all the lying and it's not like she can help, so I keep my mouth shut while she watches and try to think of other things. Mostly, for some annoying reason, my mind goes to Avery. I try to keep my feelings about it all at arm's length, so that I don't start freezing the kitchen, but I can't help remembering his face when they voted to banish Jack—the way for an instant he tried to fight for me. He looked so ill at ease there, and in spite of myself, I wonder what his life has been like, growing up in the Royal Fay Court, away from humanity, with a father who despises that human part of him.

I shake my head. Why should I care?

"Owl, where are you going?" Mom asks later, after I've spent the day slumping around school with Mallory, trying to avoid Avery and Conor.

"Am I still grounded?" It's been a week now. I look at her hopefully. I've dressed all in black for my Jack Frosting and I probably should have waited until she'd gone to bed, but honestly, I'm so tired I'd probably fall asleep and that wouldn't help anyone.

"Tell me where you're going and I'll let you know," she says, tucking her hair behind her ears. She's been working hard on her commission and there are circles under her eyes. Is she worried about me? Is that what the circles are for?

"You don't need to worry," I say, picking up my scarf. "I'm not doing anything stupid."

"Shall I be the judge of that?" she asks, looking me up and down. "I'm trying to trust you, Owl. You're not making it very easy."

"I was going to see Avery," I say, the lie coming smoothly. He'll be there anyway, after all, in his role as spy. "Just to get some fresh air for a bit . . ."

"What's he like?" she asks, leaning up against the doorjamb.

"Uh. He's got brown eyes and hair. And he's really tall. He's . . . unusual . . ." My voice trails off. I must be the color of a plum. Were those good things to say?

"And kind?"

Kind?

"Well, he's all right," I tell her. "So . . . can I go?"

"We'll call it an experiment," she says. "I'll let you go out, and I'll give you a curfew of ten, and if it all goes to plan, then we'll know."

"Know what?"

"That you can be trusted."

She leans in and gives me a great big hug and for just a moment I let myself be a kid again, comforted by her familiar smells and the rough-smooth wool of her sweater.

The next few days pass in a brittle whirl of ice and snow and school and Mallory's questioning, worried eyes. Avery doesn't say much when I encounter him on my nighttime missions, just watches me from a distance. I don't stop to talk to him. The work calls harder than anything else. It's about the only thing keeping me sane at the moment. Somehow it makes sense of everything—Jack may never accept me, but there's no question whose daughter I am when I'm out doing his work. And I need it. The harder I go at it, the more ground I cover, the better I feel—alive in a way I've never felt alive before. Every movement carries traces of magic, sending cold thrills up my spine. I go out later now. I've decided I can do without Mom's questions, so I've taken to leaving by the window in the early hours of the morning, and so far she hasn't noticed. I guess I'm getting better at it.

By the time I fall into bed I'm so tired I can barely breathe, and yet I'm wired, high on frost and a yearning to do more, do better. The church, the bridge, every major monument and a lot of the smaller ones, are glittering beneath the stars, because of me. They've never looked so beautiful. It gets hard to leave them, hard to just come home and get into my normal bed like a normal girl. I'm not normal. The thought makes me grin now, where it used to frighten me.

Who wants normal, anyway?

The lack of sleep is a bit of a problem, though. Everything revolves around my mind for hours, so that by the time I'm ready for sleep I can hardly see straight, and that's when the room starts to bustle with the noise of the owls. I think of taking down all the artwork, but they're so intent on telling me that "he does not know the truth" that I don't think it'd work. They'd just rustle at me from under the bed and that would be even more creepy.

“What do you want me to do about it?” I cry eventually. “Am I supposed to march into the Royal Court and demand answers? I don’t see that working very well! I don’t know what you mean, anyway. Jack knows the truth about me. He just doesn’t want to face it!”

“You must find him, before ’tis too late! ’Tis not his doing. ’Tis not for him to be punished for another’s manipulations! You’ll be lost to it, lost toooo-it, tu-whit . . .”

I put the pillow over my face and will myself to sleep.

36

"Owl, wait!"

I stumble over the sidewalks in the old part of town. They're slippery with ice and my toes are numb. I realize with a shock that my feet are bare and blue with cold.

But that doesn't matter, right?

"What are you doing?" Avery hisses, falling in beside me.

"My work," I say, reaching out and drawing icicles from a window ledge. Avery waits beside me while I finish, feeling satisfied when I draw my hand away to reveal a perfect row of gleaming frozen daggers.

"You don't look well," he says, frowning as he stares down at me. I wish I were taller. It's demeaning to be constantly looked down upon.

"Why are you so tall?" I demand.

"Why are you so cold?" he rallies, shaking his head then. "It's not relevant, Owl. You're doing too much. You're not looking after yourself."

"What do you care?" I ask, considering him. His copper eyes blaze in the near-dawn murk—even the freckles on his skin seem to glow.

He grabs my arm. "You're sick. You need to get home."

"I haven't finished," I murmur, stretching up to touch his hair. It looks so thick and warm. "I was going to do the lake. . . ."

"You should stop," he says, his voice strained as he jerks his head out of my reach, still holding me by the arm. "Owl, you look like a walking corpse!"

"Oh, who cares?"

"Won't your mom care?" he asks, genuine curiosity in his voice.

"She'll be fine."

I turn my back, determined to carry on with my work. He follows me around every corner and I focus harder on making ice as a distraction, pulling deeper within myself until it's rolling out of me, easy as breathing—making whole gardens white with a touch, sending streams of crystals up streetlights where they glitter, amber bright and magical. I forget that Avery is there, forget everything, running faster, faster, sending shards of ice into every dark corner.

The greenhouses in the community gardens are fragile and their roofs treacherous. I climb up carefully, balancing on the topmost ridge while frost spills down around me. One false move and I'd fall through the glass. But I won't make a false move. I move from one to another, tracing patterns on the glass, making thick, spiky ridges of ice over the metal. I can feel Avery's presence down below me and I ignore it, leaping from one greenhouse to the next until I've run out and there are only level vegetable plots before me. I jump down and move between the neat rows, all carefully sealed off. It's frustrating. Things hiding from me beneath the plastic. I prowl along, keen-eyed, looking for a mistake, for a break in the pattern. And there. There it is. A split in the smooth whiteness, fragile green fronds just visible and beneath, the soft round globes of out-of-season tomatoes. Why are they even here? Why do gardeners plant them in the winter, when they would by nature die? I reach down, my stomach sour with sudden hunger and pluck one from the thick green stem.

A bloom of condensation, a sweep of frost over the smooth red skin. It puckers and shrivels as I hold it, useless against my power. I look at it for a long time, wondering whether I feel remorse. And I realize I don't. This is nature. I am nature's work.

"What are you doing?" That infernal voice. His presence always there, reminding me of my frailties. Reminding me of his betrayal.

I turn with a glare, feathers of ice spilling out around me. He reels back with shock and I stalk from the gardens, aware that he's *still* behind me. I head for home, my head light as storm clouds gather overhead, and as I pass the park I spot the Great Oak. That looks like it could use a bit of frost. I run toward the tree.

"Owl, no!"

Avery is fast, but I'm faster, spurred on by some kind of mad determination to wind him up. I reach the oak and start to climb, leaving rimes of frost everywhere I touch. It feels amazing. The higher I get the more delicate the branches, the more beautiful the ice I lay upon it. I take my time, caressing the rough bark, feeling the power that rests within the tree. It's immense, far older than anything I've touched with frost before.

"Child, you're taking on too much. . . ." It's a rumble of a voice that resounds deep within my head and makes my stomach roll.

My feet slip on the branch and I reach out to grip the tree, but the bark seems to shift away from me and the world turns upside down. I land clumsily on the hard ground, stumbling forward as Avery reaches for me.

"Get away from me," I mutter, recovering myself as he steps away, shaking his head.

"What were you thinking?"

"Clearly I was thinking it'd be nice to fall out of a tree!" I shout, moving away from it toward the path.

"He's far too powerful for you to take on—I've told you already, you need to pace yourself!"

"Who are you to tell me what I need?"

"Who else is going to tell you?" he shouts. "You're doing too much. You're not looking after the human part of you!" His copper eyes blaze in the darkness, and even the freckles on his skin seem to glow. "You cannot *be* Jack Frost," he continues. "You're a human, a *girl*. There's a balance, it's important. . . . You need to remember that."

"How can I forget with you around?"

"I'm trying to *help*!"

"I don't need your help—what do you know anyway? All you've got to control is a few stupid *leaves*. Even a *kid* could do that!"

Ice blooms out across the grass as I shout, and Avery staggers back until he can't outpace it anymore. Instead he's forced to stand on it. He doesn't look too comfortable there, I think with satisfaction.

"You think that's all there is to autumn? To me? Are

you really that blind, Owl?" He skates toward me, his face mutinous. I step back, suddenly aware of how tall he is, how angular. There's a wiry strength in him that I'd never really thought about before.

"Everything autumn touches dies," he snarls. "Do you know how much control I have to use every time I'm around you or one of your stupid human friends?"

"Avery!"

He raises his hands and his eyes blaze. The trees around us lower their branches, the remaining green leaves swiftly turning to an amber and gold that gleams. Another second and they're falling, dry brown husks that skitter across the ice.

"Stop it!" I shout as he starts toward me. In that instant there are traces of the Earl in his expression, something dark and inhuman that looks right through me and won't stop, won't give in, not for anything. "*Avery!*"

He flinches and stops in his tracks, tipping his head to the sky as he takes a deep, shuddering breath. The trees are released.

"I can stop any time I want to," he says, taking another step toward me. "Can you?"

"Just go, Avery. Just leave me *alone*!"

I put my hands out to push him back and hail begins to fall, hitting at him. He lowers his head, fighting through it as my head starts to spin. I *am* doing too much, I realize, as everything gets hazy. I try to pull it back but I can't, everything's unravelling.

"Owl . . ."

"Uh."

"Wake up. You need to get back in."

In? In where?

I open my eyes to see Avery looming over me. I shrink back, looking around. The sky is lightening with dawn. We're sitting on the step outside my front porch, I realize, a wave of nausea rolling over me.

"Your mom . . . she'll find out you've been out. I didn't know how to get you through the window. . . ." He looks up as he says it, as if he genuinely spent some time considering how to do just that. "She'll mind, won't she? If you're not home and she realizes?"

"Yeah, she'll mind," I whisper, pulling myself up and digging my keys out of my pocket. "Won't yours?"

"Mine?" He looks away. "No. I've, uh . . . I've always lived in the Royal Court. With the Earl." He takes a breath, looks me in the eye. "I'm sorry for what happened."

"Right."

"Take the day off," he says. "Tell your mom you're sick or something. You can do that, yes?"

"Why would I?"

"I told you, you're overdoing it," he says. "You don't understand what that could do—"

"I understand fine, thank you," I interrupt him. "And I don't have any choice, do I? You'll tell them if I start falling behind, if I can't keep up with my work. And then they'll know Jack's daughter is failing and that won't help either of us."

He bites his lip. "I'm not going to tell them anything," he says, shaking his head. "It's not your work, Owl. I think we should get him back. This whole thing was a mistake. . . ."

"I don't want him back."

What did he ever do for me, anyway?

"You need him. If you carry on like this, you're going to lose yourself. I think you already are. . . ."

Avery knows things I don't. And I wonder—what if the owls in my bedroom are right? What if there *is* some big secret that could answer everything and help me see clearly? Do I even want that? I don't want to go back to how things were before.

"I just can't," I tell the wooden owl. "I won't."

Even if it is a little more frightening, now that I've seen how Avery can change. That inhuman force of power we *both* have.

I remember how Jack and the North Wind played

on the ice that day, how horrified Avery was. I think I understand a little better now. If they took it just a step further, how destructive it would be . . . but I won't think about that.

Because they didn't.

In the morning Mom makes me take some painkillers, washed down with orange juice that stings my throat. She gets the extra blanket, the scratchy yellow one some old ancestor knitted back in the dawn of time, and puts it over my quilt.

"What have you been doing, little Owl?" she whispers as the owl on the bedpost winks at me.

"Little Owl," I murmur. "That's what he called me, 'fore they sent him away. . . ."

"Who, my love, who?"

She sounds just like an owl, I think, as my eyelids grow heavy.

37

I open my eyes.

And blink.

And I'm dreaming.

Or it's a weird sort of nightmare, like the one where you're naked in class.

It's my bedroom, so far pretty normal. And Mallory is sitting on the end of the bed, which is a bit surprising but not completely outrageous. And then Avery is here, perched awkwardly on the little wicker chair by the window, and that's just impossible.

I close my eyes again, but now I can hear them talking, having a heated discussion about night visits to strange woodlands and Jack Frost's banishment and my new role as Mini-Frost.

Eventually I have to open my eyes again. They don't

seem to be going anywhere, and it's annoying having to listen to them talk about me without saying anything.

"Now you're in trouble," whispers the owl on the bedpost with a soft clack of her wooden wings. I sit up and Mallory and Avery turn to stare at me—which is incredibly unsettling, especially since I've no idea how long I've been asleep or what on earth I look like.

"What are you doing in my bedroom?" I demand.

"We were with your mom, and then you started shouting about secrets and lies, and so *I* came to check on you because she was a bit tangled up with the pasta maker," Mallory says earnestly. "And Avery followed me . . ."

"And then you thought you'd both just stay in here and talk about me while I was sleeping? Isn't that a bit weird?"

"He burst in after me and wouldn't go away," Mallory says, glaring at Avery. "I called out to your mom that you were fine, but he stayed anyway. . . . He says he was worried. Your mom seems to like him. . . ." She shrugs and mouths a "sorry" at me.

I look at the window and imagine making my escape, but I don't. I just get out of bed, glance in the mirror, nearly have a heart attack at the state of my hair, chuck a big sweater on over my clothes, and sit down to face the music.

Just as the owls on the walls begin to kick up a fuss.

"They *speak* to you?" Mallory asks, as she and Avery look up at the drawings, neither of them able to hide their shock.

"Not always," I say tiredly, knowing I should say more to explain it and not having the words. I focus on Avery instead. "Why are you here?" I demand.

"He says you're in real trouble!" Mallory exclaims, her eyes wide with horror, turning from the pictures. "Owl, you've been sick for days, and he says if we don't sort this out you might just . . . disappear!"

"Days?"

"Well, two days . . ."

"Then who's been doing the work? I need to get out there!" I start scrambling up from the bed, but Avery puts a hand on my arm.

"No," he says. "It's not a good idea."

"Why not? It's what I promised!" I want it. I need it. My hands are shaking with the need for it. I sit on them, but my blood is restless and I know I can't just sit here like this for long.

"You haven't been looking after yourself," he says, shaking his head. "I should have warned you properly before. I tried. . . . I wasn't sure what to say. . . ."

"It's serious, Owl," Mallory insists. "He says if you carry on like this you'll never be the same!"

"I'll be fine," I say, looking out of the window again.

It's sunset and there's not a sign of frost out there. "Did winter stop because I didn't do it?"

"No," he says with a withering look. "Winter isn't constant like that, you know that much. It's a mild spell. . . ."

"So I should get back out there."

"No," says Mallory. "It's changing you, Owl. It's like . . . you've embraced the part of you that's Jack Frost, which nobody blames you for doing . . . but it's sort of, uh, showing. We know things are different now, but we still want you to be you."

"I am me!"

"But if you're to live in this human world, you must retain your humanity," Avery says. "Balancing the two is difficult. You're failing."

"Oh, and you're so successful, walking around so normal with your glinty eyes and your extreme height, and all the wind and the leaves. . . ."

"I never said I was *normal*," he says. "Being half human and half fay isn't easy. But I've had a lifetime to learn balance. There are dangers. . . ."

"What dangers?"

"You'll fall between," he says. "No longer existing in this world or in the other. You'll be without a human body, able to see and hear everything, but invisible, voiceless."

A chill prickles over my shoulders.

"It's easy to get caught up in the magic of it all," Avery explains. "Being Jack's daughter you're half elemental, so even among fay your power will be strong. Probably making it even more difficult to manage."

"I'm managing fine!" I say.

"But if you forget to look after your human side then you won't be," Avery says.

"So what do we do?" Mallory asks.

"We get Jack back," Avery says. "He's the only one who can teach Owl how to use what he gave her with caution. And when he's back she won't feel so obliged to do his work all the time."

"I am still here!" I snap.

"Barely," Avery retorts.

"I don't want him back! He won't come, anyway. He doesn't accept that I'm his daughter—and he's been banished, thanks to the Queen and your father! Why does he hate him so much, anyway? What was this grudge? How can it possibly have led to all this?"

He shrugs. "I don't know. It goes back a long way. Probably to do with power. The Earl is in his power for a short time compared to Jack. And then, you know, Jack's kind of famous! Who ever heard of the Earl of October?" He smiles, but it's a funny self-mocking thing, and when I meet his eye I can see how hard it is for him to talk about his father. I try to focus on what he's said and think about how quickly the leaves turn brown and fall from the trees in autumn. Is that the Earl's problem? That winter comes too soon, steps on his toes? "Jack'll come back," Avery says. "He can fight the banishment, we just need to go to his domain and explain things to him. How did your mom get to him? Was there something in that old storybook you mentioned? Do you have it? I can get to my father's place anytime, but I don't know Jack's world. . . ."

"I've already tried it." I fold my arms. "It didn't work."

"You have the spell, then," he says. "It'll work now. I know how to cast it."

"And who is going to go on this trip?" asks Mallory. "Just you two?"

"I never said I was going to go!" I say. "It's a hare-brained idea. Everything's fine."

"But is it?" Mallory asks. "If Avery's right about the danger you're in, then I think you should go, Owl. You need Jack's help."

I crouch down and haul the book out from under the bed, blowing the dust off the cover and ignoring Avery's outraged look. He virtually snatches it from me, leafing through the ancient pages with reverence.

"I should be able to get myself through," he says eventually in a subdued voice. "Maybe I should go alone. . . ."

"Shouldn't we all go?" Mallory asks.

"You won't be able to," Avery says. "When Isolde went through there was . . ." He clears his throat. "There was a particular force at work. I can't recreate that. I can get myself through, and Owl will get through if she's accepted her elemental side—which I think we can all agree she has done."

"What are you hiding?" I demand. "What's this thing that's going to convince him to come back? It won't be me. I already tried. And now . . . now we don't need him anyway! I can do this!" Ice begins to spread over my scalp and I take a deep breath, trying to hold it back, curling my hands into fists as frost sweeps over my skin.

"Not for much longer," Avery says in a firm voice, seeing everything. "And Jack has to come back anyway, to clear his name."

"Clear his name?"

"Your . . . existence . . . wasn't only down to Jack and your mom," he says, his eyes still on the book. A blush of color rushes up his neck. "The Earl gave his power to the spell when Isolde read it out, enabling her to get through to Jack's world. My father wanted to create you, so that he'd have something over Jack. . . ."

The room seems to get smaller, darker. Mallory's warm hand reaches for mine. Avery closes the book and keeps his head low. The owls screech. They knew it all along. The Earl engineered it so that I would be born, to my father's shame. That's what he was talking with the Queen about that day in the forest: this is the trap they set for Jack.

I am the trap.

"I'm sorry," Avery says, his voice soft. "I thought you should know. I thought it would help you understand. They've waited a long time for this to play out. A long time in human years, that is. To them it's nothing—"

"Go," I whisper, pulling myself away from Mallory. "Go and help Mom or something. I need a moment."

"But, Owl . . ." Mallory begins.

"*Go!*" It comes out as a hiss, the room instantly plummeting in temperature. Mallory's breath puffs out like steam as she shuffles away from me, getting clumsily to her feet.

"Don't do this," Avery says, rising from the chair. "You need help, Owl."

"I said *GO!*" I breathe, unsurprised when a flurry of fine ice crystals escape my mouth. Avery shies away. "I just need a *moment*."

"That's fine," he says, coming toward me, his copper eyes blazing. "Have your *moment*, but don't think I'm going anywhere until this is sorted. You're a danger, and not only to yourself."

With that he sweeps toward the door, shoving Mallory

before him, a brisk wind curling in his wake, ice crystals spinning in the air.

There was an owl in Mom's story. She was the creature of wisdom, the one who told her that she would forever keep a part of this magical world with her, something to hold on to when everything else was gone.

She meant me. My mother knew it somehow, even named me after her. But did that owl know I was only a pawn in the Earl's game? That one day I would be used against my father?

The owls in the bedroom rustle and flutter on their pages around me, whispering of winter worlds and isolated souls who do not know the truth. "He does not know it all, Owl! This is not his doing," they murmur.

"He doesn't know that it was all the Earl's doing? That I'm just part of some . . . evil plan? Did you know?" I glare at the wooden owl, but it refuses to stir, and the flocks that adorn my walls are suddenly silent. I look at them anew. The earliest are done in crayon, framed by Mom, the latter ones in charcoal, the details more vivid. Every single one now seems so naive and hopeful. The owl did nothing to help my father against the Earl that day at the Royal Court, though she must have known.

I grab the dusty old suitcase from the top of my wardrobe and pull it down, heaving it on to my bed, opening the leather straps. Then I turn to the walls. I'm so tired of it all. It shouldn't be possible, not any of it, and yet it is and there they are, my own drawings rustling and snapping their feathered wings, clacking their sharp beaks like living, breathing creatures.

They've done me no favors, in spite of all their fuss.

The framed ones are the easiest. I whisk them from their hooks, throw them into the suitcase, satisfied when they clatter against one another, glass cracking. The owls within the charcoal pictures watch me with wide eyes as I peel them from the walls. My fingers are shaking, my skin is covered in ice, and yet not one of them rips as I pull them down, haphazardly rolling the larger ones, shoving them all into the suitcase. They've been there so long, some of them, that they leave their own imprint on the wall, even after they've been torn down. Pale squares framed in dark lines.

"Does that make you feel better?" asks the owl on the bedpost, after I've closed the suitcase and thrust it clumsily back up onto the wardrobe.

"No," I whisper, my feet crunching over ice as I make for the window. I look back at the room, my breath catching in my throat at the layer of frost over every surface. "No, it doesn't."

I had intended to leave through the window. The branches of the ash tree in the front garden knock against the glass, reminding me that it's time to go out into the world, lose myself in Jack's work.

"Owls are birds of prey," says the wooden owl. "They do not flee. They fight."

I sink down onto the windowsill, putting my knuckles up against my teeth, squeezing my eyes shut.

All I wanted was a father.

Warm hands pull me away from the windowsill. Avery, steadying me as I stumble, watching as I struggle not to fall apart.

"I'm so angry," I whisper.

"I know," he says, after a long pause. "I know what that feels like."

"Do you?" I pull away, look up at him.

"I'll never know my mother," he says, a little twist in his mouth. "I'll never fit—in the Royal Court or at school."

"What happened to your mother?"

"She wasn't like yours," he says, his jaw clenching. "She couldn't accept what had happened, what I was. She was afraid of me and it . . . she was . . . The Earl saw what was happening and took me away from her."

"She let you go?"

"He says she was relieved." He shrugs. "I'll never know now. She died."

I stare at him, my heart pounding. His copper eyes are on fire and I want to know more. I want to know how he felt, what his life was like with his mother and then with his father, in the Royal Court. Had he known what he was before he walked into that place with the Earl? Was he afraid? Does he think of her often? Avery looks away after a moment and I bite my lip.

"I'm sorry. . . ." I manage eventually.

He takes a deep breath, shakes his head. "Anyway. Now you know. So are you ready?"

"Ready?"

"To do this . . ."

"No! I'm not going, Avery. This is what I *am* now. I don't want to change. It's not so bad. I'll get better at balancing things. If you can do it then so can I."

"I've had all my life to learn! While you were listening to bedtime stories safely tucked up here, I was up in the branches of the Green Man, painting his leaves red. I was being lectured by the Lady on harmony, playing hide-and-seek with the tree-sprites, learning how cruel they can be—and how kind . . ."

"And now what? It's too late for me? I just have to run to *him* to beg for help? Can't you teach me?"

"No," he says. "It's too late for that. You've already gone deeper than I ever have. They always told me, if you stop listening to your human body, that's it, there is no return. This is what they meant, Owl. One more night out like that and you might be lost forever."

I stare at him. He stares back. He's not going to change his mind. But neither am I. I'm tired of being lectured, tired of doing all I can and still it's never enough. I crave the bitter night air, the clarity of starlight on darkened streets, and I'm about to open the window behind me when Mom's voice breaks in, the warmth and normality of it like a shock against my tired, frustrated mind.

"Dinner!"

Part Three

38

Avery is so quiet over dinner. He keeps looking at Mom with these haunted eyes as she buzzes around the kitchen, bangles tinkling, bringing little dishes of olives, parmesan, tomatoes, lighting candles, talking about her work with Mallory and asking him questions about school, family. He murmurs the briefest answers, looking away whenever she looks at him. I wonder if he even remembers his own mother.

He and Mallory keep exchanging glances. When I dust my cutlery with ice I can see how they notice, how they flinch. Even Mom starts watching me more closely after a while, picking up on the tension at the table. And then it's too much. I make my excuses and dash to my room, my head buzzing, only to be followed by both of them minutes later.

"Don't you think you should go home?" I ask peevishly, staring at them from under my hat.

"No," says Mallory, lighting candles.

"What are you doing?"

"You're doing this," she says. "Avery, get the book, let's get started."

"Mallory!"

"I'm not losing you too," she says. Her voice wobbles, but she refuses to look at me, just keeps darting around with the matches.

"Oh, Mall . . ."

"Just do it, Owl," she says fiercely, sitting next to me on the bed, her eyes sparkling. "At least try!"

I look from her to Avery as he joins us on the bed. He pulls the book onto his lap and reaches for my hand, and even if I don't think it's going to work I find I can't say no. He doesn't hesitate, his eyes blaze as he starts to read the incantation, his voice deep and melodic. The words get slower as he goes and the buzzing in my head seems to intensify. Suddenly a shudder of something silver bright goes through me and I feel myself falling, falling, my stomach lurching, then there's the sharp tang of crisp outdoor air in my nostrils, hard earth beneath my feet.

Winter cuts sharp and true across my face as I open my eyes to see, all around me, the world my mother described so many times, soothing me to sleep with the magic in her voice. I realize I'm in exactly the same place she came to, all that time ago: "*in the clearing between the trees that towered out in every direction: black with bark and white with frost.*"

And my father found her here, as she turned and turned again, waiting for something to become familiar.

"*Nothing was familiar.*"

The air aches with the bleakness of winter, and when I look up I half expect to see my father there, his dark hair thick with frost. I turn, and turn again, hoping to see him and hoping not to. And all around me is only the stark silence of looming, skeletal trees beneath a pearl-bright sky.

"Owl?"

Avery. His voice is fractured, grating against the silence. It sounds like he's been calling for hours. I turn again, eyes searching for him between the narrow trunks of the trees.

"Avery?"

There's a scuffling sound and he emerges, breath steaming in the air. He's different here: taller, broader, his hair a flame against the black and white.

"I've been looking for you," he says, his voice uncertain as he comes toward me. His copper eyes glint as he looks me up and down. His footsteps are unsteady. "This place . . . distorts things. I feel like I've been here for days already." The shadow of a smile flickers at his lips. "I haven't been, have I?"

"No," I say, reaching out as he stumbles. "But time passes differently here, I think. Mom always said . . . Have you been wandering for days?" Between his hair and his eyes he's pale with cold, and there's something haunted in his face, something that suggests he's been where he should never have been. No matter how angry I am with him it's painful to see. "Go back, Avery. You don't look like you belong here."

"You do," he says, pulling away from me and leaning up against one of the trees. "You look like a part of it all already."

"Perhaps I am," I say, looking down at myself. My skin is the color of the purest just-laid frost, it gleams in the pale sunlight that filters through the wooded glade. "What do we do now?"

"Find Jack . . . " His eyes are full of doubts. "Will you? I've got you this far, but now that we're here, I can't . . . I'm not sure what comes next. I couldn't even find my way out of this glade." He looks up. The trees reach their brittle branches way up high into the sky, bending only slightly in the breeze. "It's not like anywhere I've been before, Owl, it pulls at me— "

"Let's get out of here," I say, reaching for him again.

I tuck my hand through his arm and pull him forward through trees that start to whisper around us, as a pale wind moves through them. "Is that you?"

"Is what me?" he asks, his eyes still looking upward.

"The wind."

"Oh! Might be. Who knows?"

"Avery, snap out of it!" I say. It's like pulling a dead weight, like all the will has gone out of him. We reach the edge of the glade, finally, pushing our way through the tightly packed trees as roots twist in the ground, reaching for our feet. It must be some kind of defense, to stop interlopers getting through to whatever else is out there. I get the feeling that without me Avery really would have just wandered forever. I didn't realize. Mom's stories were all about the magic and the beauty. They didn't give enough idea of the danger.

I push my way through dark, thorny vines, the stark silence making my head spin. Avery follows silently behind me, his hand in mine, and then we're through, out into the open air of a world all blue and white. Before I have time to look around, my feet give way beneath me and suddenly I'm careening down a snow-covered hill toward a frozen, ice-blue lake. I lose Avery along the way, tumbling head over heels, eventually landing in a spray of snow on top of the lake. The ice creaks ominously beneath my weight but it doesn't give. The sky is a pale bruise overhead, glowing yellow over in the west.

"Avery?" I sit up. "Where are you?"

"H-h-h . . ."

I frown, standing to look for him, as a mound of snow at the bottom of the hill rears up and explodes, revealing a blue-lipped Avery.

"Are you all right?" I demand, making my way over to him, my bare feet firm on the ice. He steps toward me and immediately slips, landing flat on his back with a grunt. I've never seen him so clumsy. It must be something in the nature of Jack's world that works against him even as it stirs in my veins, making me feel stronger than ever.

"I don't know," he says, staring up at me. His features are taut in the winter glow, his copper eyes dazed as his teeth begin to chatter. We're both dressed in the light clothes we were wearing in the apartment and it's clearly not going to be enough for him here.

"Get up," I say, reaching down and steadying him as he slips on the ice. "Take my sweater." I pull it over my head and try to give it to him, but he thrusts an arm out and swipes it away.

"No, thank you," he mutters, keeping his head down. "It won't fit anyway. I'm fine." He pulls away from me and moves forward over the ice, his back hunched, breaths coming quick and hard.

"Are you sure? We shouldn't have done this, Avery. We should never have come here! What were you thinking?"

"Couldn't carry on like you were . . . and we're here now. We need to find . . ." He frowns, looking up. "Who was it?"

"Jack!" My voice rings out with frustration, which is mostly born out of fear. He's like a shadow of himself. My heart thuds in my chest as I remember what he said about the dangers. Is this how it happens? Is he losing himself, all because he came here? All because of me? All because I was embracing who I'm supposed to be?

"Jack, Jack, Jack!" My father's name rings out all around us and I turn, heart racing, but it's only an echo of my own voice, a brittle sound that makes snow slide from the hills.

"That's right." Avery nods, pushing himself forward along the ice. "Jack."

"Avery." I stop him with a hand on his chest. "Go home. You don't need to be here. I'm not even sure why we *are* here, and your father will be furious."

"He's always furious," he murmurs, his eyes fixed on the horizon. He moves my hand away and starts forward again, his movements dogged. "Doesn't mean he's right. He thought you'd be easier to deal with than Jack. Weaker." He looks sidelong at me. "He was wrong.

People. People are more different than I thought." His voice slurs. "They're scornful of humans at the Royal Court. I thought it would all be jealousy and pride . . . destruction. But at school . . . I see the way you laugh, the way you look after one another. All the other stuff's there too, but the way you all live, I've never known that . . . all that time you spend with one another, fighting, hoping, trying to make something with what little time you have . . ."

I steady him as he slips again on the ice and search the horizon for signs of Jack's house. Something. Anything. But stretching out in every direction is only more ice, and frozen hills to either side, gray mountains rearing up behind them. Didn't Mom speak of goats and eagles? There are no signs of life here at all, and I have no way of knowing if we're heading in the right direction.

This is Jack's world. He must know, somehow, that we're here. Why doesn't he come?

"JACK!" I shout at the top of my voice. Avery startles beside me, jolted from his dreamlike state as the call brings snow tumbling down onto the ice. There's no way Jack can't have heard it, but there's no response as the echoes subside. Only more silence.

And then a sound that hurts my ears and makes my heart stutter.

A desperate, keening howl that echoes endlessly and makes yet more snow crash from the hills around us, cascading down and spilling over the ice in a great white tide.

The wolves of winter.

39

Running over ice, Avery beside me, slipping and sliding. I can feel the presence of the wolves through the prickle in my neck, the shudder that rings out as more snow falls onto the frozen lake. They're stalking us from the hills above, their every move triggering yet more avalanches. If they overtake us, we'll be buried in snow.

There's another sorrowful howl, closer this time. I risk a look back as Avery collides with me, his feet slipping from beneath him. Five narrow gray shapes are darting down the hillside, bounding onto the ice, their claws scrabbling for purchase. Even at a distance I can see they're far bigger than I'd ever imagined. They must be at least as tall as me at the shoulder.

I grab at Avery, pulling him up, cursing and pushing him toward the edge of the ice where there's a thin lip of snow. "We need to keep running!"

"I c-can't . . ." He shivers, his lips blue. "G-going to slow you down." He gives me a shove. "Go on without me. . . ."

"I'm not leaving you here!"

"You h-have to."

His face is startlingly pale. He seems to run out of breath even as he tries to speak. I pull at him, but I'm not sure he could move if he wanted to.

"Avery! Come on!"

The wolves are hurtling toward us, their muscles bunching effortlessly as they run. A low growl seems to ricochet off the snow itself.

"Snap out of it!" I hiss desperately, my mind racing. "Please, Avery—mind over matter, tell yourself it's warm, or you're wearing an invisible coat or something. . . ."

"An-n-n-vis'ble coat?"

"Yes! Something—anything!" I pull at him again as I say it, picking up my pace and hoping for some miracle. A hidden track, a cave, anything but this open expanse of winter that seems out to kill us one way or the other. Avery frowns, breaking into a lurching run at my side, but it's no good, there's nowhere to run or hide.

In desperation I shout out, my voice rising above the growls of the wolves, as if I can push them back with my fear alone. At my cry, great channels of snow begin to pour from the mountains onto the ice, engulfing us all in a winter storm. I can't breathe, can't see. Ice fills my mouth and nose, plasters my hair back from my skull. It's like being in a roaring white room, booming and shuddering, everything else completely obliterated. I push back against it, raising my hands and trying to keep us from being buried alive, creating a kind of bubble. Snow shoots off around us in all directions, but inside the bubble it is still and silent. I take a deep breath, shaking with relief as Avery looks up, amazed, at the invisible shield.

Then a heavy weight lands on my right shoulder, claws digging in, warmth brushing up against my ear. I bite back a shriek, imagining it's one of the wolves, about to go for the kill, and stagger back, my breath like fire in my lungs.

"So," says the great white owl when I turn my head, her golden eyes glowing. "You are come into your heritage at last."

The wolves shake themselves vigorously as the avalanche settles around them, their fur standing in spikes coated with ice, their eyes still fixed on me. My whole body is reverberating with the shock of it all, but I stand straight, the owl still on my shoulder, as Avery struggles to his feet beside me.

"Are you all right?" I whisper.

"H-hmm." He nods through chattering teeth.

"I didn't mean to do that. . . ."

"You did this?"

"She is Jack's daughter," says the owl. "She has power here. Power enough to bring winter down upon you all." She glares at the wolves, who have gathered closer together. "Do you think you can stand against her?"

"She is not of this world," one of the wolves says, stepping forward. He's bigger than the others, his muzzle grizzled white. "How are we to tolerate her?"

"Tolerate her? If Jack is your master then this is your mistress. . . ."

"She is a false mistress—even he does not accept her."

"She's his daughter, all the same," says Avery in a low voice.

"And who are you, to be here? To speak thus?"

Two of the wolves begin to creep forward, their backs low, teeth bared.

"He's here with me," I say, stepping forward until I'm nose to nose with the alpha wolf, standing firm despite the shivers running up my spine. The owl ruffles her wings, beating into my hair, making me start.

"We do not recognize your right to be here," growls the wolf. "And he is not a creature of winter at all, it is forbidden."

One of the wolves takes a flying leap toward Avery. I

shout out, and the owl thrusts herself up into the sky with a shriek, powerful white wings sweeping through the bitter cold. I rush to the wolf, grabbing at its dense warm fur, trying to turn it from its course. I'm too late to stop the hit. Huge paws strike Avery's chest and throw him back onto the ice. In desperation I grab at his shoulder, pulling him toward me as ice builds in my veins, staring at the wolves and daring them, just daring them to get closer, to fight me here where my power is at its greatest.

I can feel it now: the connection between myself and this place, this land that my father built for himself.

Strands of bright, ice-cold magic stretch like a web around me, power ready to be taken. I brace myself and expand my chest, letting it fill me. It gathers on my skin, through my hair, thicker and sharper than ever. Avery stirs and I draw him closer to me with one hand, while the other builds storm clouds in the sky. Suddenly there it is, a hard blizzard of ice and hail, striking out around us, making the wolves step back. I draw farther away from them and the ice quakes beneath my feet, rising up, a great sweep of blue-white that carries us, farther and faster, away from them. Away from their shock and fear, away from their mournful, accusing eyes. The tide rips through the lake as it goes, and the gray-white world where my father hides is full of the sound of ice forming and crashing, forming and crashing, over and over again.

I ride the wave as if it's the only thing that matters, as if I could keep going forever, my blood surging in my veins, Avery beside me, snow falling all around, the wolves now just little dark shapes behind.

"OWL!"

I lurch as that inhuman voice breaks the air around us. Suddenly Jack is there, riding on my wave, the owl wheeling past high overhead. He doesn't look so tall now. He doesn't look so inhuman. The look on his face, of shock and almost fear, is a look I've seen before on other faces.

"Stop this." He holds out a hand to me. His hair is blown back by the speed of our progress and I grin at him as I urge it onward, onward. "Little Owl, what are you doing? Stop!" He looks down, alarmed, as the lake is eaten up by my splintered, jagged wave of ice. He makes a sweeping gesture with one hand and the snow instantly stops, clouds unfurling to reveal a pale, cold sky. I frown and raise my hand.

"NO!" he howls, making the air shudder. "Look! Look at what you're doing. You'll destroy yourself. You'll destroy everything!"

"What do you care?" I demand. "You can build it all up again, can't you? You can fix it! Surely I'm no match for *Jack Frost*?"

"I can't fix *you*!" he snarls. "I can't bring your boy

back to life if you've killed him!"

What?

I look down at Avery, who is kneeling, his head pressed against my legs. Perhaps he was trying to shelter from the snow. Perhaps he was trying to get warmth from my body.

But my body isn't warm. It's ice, through and through.

"Avery?"

He doesn't stir. I stoop, shaking at his shoulder. There's a handprint where I've been holding on to him and as I shake he slumps forward and the back of his neck is exposed. It's covered in frost, the outline of his spine sparkling as it catches the light.

What have I done?

My heart seems to fall through my chest as I lose momentum and the wave tilts with a horrendous screech, thundering, hammering. I struggle to keep myself upright, struggle to keep hold of his frozen shirt. His skin is blue white.

And it shouldn't be.

He is the warmth of autumn, the red gold of fallen leaves, the glossy brown of bright new chestnuts. His copper eyes are like fire when he's angry.

What have I done?

The ice collapses around us in a vast white avalanche. I can't see anything. I can't feel anything. I'm floundering in a sea of icy mist, tumbling head over heels in a dreamlike slow motion, Avery being tossed around next to me. I keep my fingers tight against his shirt, try to soften his fall, and then, just as we hit the ground, a searing brightness blinds me. I blink, and when I open my eyes everything is still again, everything as it should be. The wide, frozen lake, the pale sky above. Jack, stalking through his domain. He reaches out and I feel a surge of relief at the look of regret that softens his angular features as he looks down, then I realize it's not for me.

He pulls Avery gently away from me, lifts him into his arms, and turns his back.

"Are you coming?" he demands, his voice cold. He strides toward a low dome on the horizon, as the pale fingers of a rose-gold sunset begin to stretch across the sky. I stumble to my feet, slipping on the ice, trying to keep up, my eyes fixed on Avery, willing him to move, willing it so hard that little sparks appear in the corners of my eyes. But he is motionless in my father's arms, and I can hardly breathe myself, because I did this. *I* did this.

What have I become?

40

The coldest thing in my father's home is me.

The most frightening thing is Avery.

Jack is gentle. Jack is kind—when it comes to saving the life of the son of a mortal enemy. He lays Avery on a rough wooden bench laden with furs and stokes the fire until it seems that, surely, surely his home will collapse around us in a flood of thawed ice. It doesn't. The room quickly warms and I loiter by the door and watch and wait for Avery to stir.

"Will he be all right?" My voice is splintered, a husk of a voice. I cringe as I hear it, but I continue anyway, because I need to know. "I mean, this place . . . he can't just . . . he can't die here, can he?" I can't move from the door. I don't know what to do. What can I possibly do, after all this? Should I just slink into the nearest hole and stay there, away from the world? Is that what Jack does here? Is it remorse for his cruelty that keeps him here? All the life he has ended, whether it's large or small—it must take its toll.

"He is as frail as any human. His body has limits," he says, his silver eyes boring into me. "And you've just about killed him. You see here . . ." He pulls back the blankets, exposing Avery's shoulder: a handprint burned into his pale skin, pale skin that gets paler, more translucent even as I look. "His spirit is weak, it dims. I am not sure that bodily warmth will be enough."

"Then what? What do we do?"

"We hope." He shrugs. "And we get him home."

I nod. "I didn't think you would be so . . . that you would care . . ."

"I would not see the son of the Earl die on my watch. Whatever their faults, neither of them deserves that."

I stare at him, unnerved by his attitude. We seem to be the wrong way around. He's supposed to be doing the damage. I'm supposed to be stopping him. Isn't that how it is? How it was? Have I changed that much?

"Isn't it about nature? Survival?" I ask haltingly.

"He should not have been here!" Jack roars, his eyes blazing.

"He wouldn't have been if you had stayed and fought harder!" I shout back, the words tearing themselves out of me, hot and heavy. "He brought me here to get you back! He said we had to come, or I'd be lost between worlds. He said I was doing too much, but I couldn't stop. . . ."

"Who said you should be doing my work anyway?" he demands.

"It was a choice," I say. "When you left, the Queen told me I couldn't just go home. I had to stay in the Royal Court forever, or I could go out and do as you did . . . and so what else was I supposed to do? You just marched off. You left me there!" My throat tightens. "Everyone else could see the truth of who I am. Why wouldn't you? Am I so awful?"

He frowns, and the temperature of the room drops.

"Why would you say such a thing?"

"You abandoned me! You refused to acknowledge me, even though it's obvious what I am!" I feel reckless, determined to get through to him no matter what the consequences. I need him to see me, to really *see* me. "Are you afraid?" I demand.

"I am not!" he bursts out, standing taller, the windows creaking with ice. He's gray white, bleak as snow clouds, his jaw lined with ice, his hair thick with it. His silver eyes blaze and thick strands of ice begin to travel up the walls, like the gnarled trunks of trees.

"So then *what*?"

"I cannot have a daughter!" he says. Ice creeps across the ceiling and I shouldn't have done it, I shouldn't have wound him up. Avery will freeze. "It isn't possible!"

"Okay," I say in a small voice, sitting heavily on the bench across from Avery. I barely feel the heat of the fire, I'm so tired, so bewildered by everything that has happened. I watch Avery's chest rise and fall and tell myself nothing else matters. I need to get him home. I need to make it all better.

"It was a dream I had," Jack sighs, sitting next to me. "Of the woman. Of a life I could only ever look in on. I was always on the outside, in your world. Watching families snuggle in their homes, away from my games. It was never something *I* could have. I am not human. I cannot be a father!"

"But you are," I say numbly, still watching Avery. "The Earl sent my mother to you. She was as real as I am now."

He fixes his eyes on me.

"It was *real*?"

I nod, my throat too tight for words, noticing all the other strangely homely touches in the room: a snow globe of London on the mantelpiece, a bone-white china mug on the small table by the fire, a thick pile rug before it. The staircase is ornate, the spindles carved to look like the trunks of trees. For all his otherness, all his refusal to care about life, he has made a home here.

"But it can't have been," Jack breathes. "It isn't possible. It isn't in the natural order of things. . . . " He stands and begins to pace up and down, running his hands through his hair. "She was real," he mutters. "The wolves said she did not belong. I thought . . . I thought it was a dream. I never let myself consider . . ." He shakes his head. "How can this be?"

"The Earl had something to do with the spell she used."

"The Earl has always detested me," he says. "He has done all this, used you, to be rid of me!"

"Now that you know the truth you can tell them!" I say, tears gathering in my eyes. "They'll have to pardon you, and you can come back. I can't do it, Jack. All this"—I gesture at Avery—"all this is my fault. I got lost in it. I can't *do* it the way you do!"

"I'm not coming back," he says quietly, watching while I swipe ice from my cheeks. "Why should I? People don't know who I am, what I do for them! And I will not go before those who accused me and beg for justice. The Earl may have manipulated this, but it is not all his doing. The Royal Court is swayed by these notions of power. It has been corrupted by humanity's flaws. . . ."

"People *do* know your name," I tell him, my head aching. "People know what you do. There are legends about you. There have been for hundreds of years. There's poetry, movies, children's stories, legends in old books . . ."

"About me?" His eyes brighten with sudden delight. I remember the time I saw him play-fighting with the North Wind. He is different in his own world, but only by degrees. He's still fickle, playful. He'll never be who I wanted him to be, all those years I was imagining my father. He swings from despair to glee in an instant. He's a child. What did I expect? How's he going to help anything?

"Yes," I sigh. "They know what you do for them."

"They believe in me? If I walked among them they would know who I am?"

"Well . . ." I hesitate. "I mean, they believe in you deep down. They see what you do, and they admire it."

"And you have been doing my work all this time?"

"I tried to," I say. "Avery says I was consumed . . . He said I would disappear."

Jack looks uneasily at Avery. I realize I can see the lines of the settee through him and my heart sinks. "But you have not."

"No," I reply. "He said I needed you back, to teach me . . ."

"It's not easy to straddle two worlds," Jack says, sitting beside me, staring into the fireplace. "I am sorry for you, little Owl, but I won't return. I shall stay here."

"Don't you care about what happens to me at all?"

"I have already intervened for you," he says. "I knew you were here the moment you arrived. I let you make your way. I let you stand against the wolves. I saw that you are as much of this world as the other." He grimaces. "I *did* see that. And you tell me the Earl intervened all those years ago, that the woman . . . your mother . . . was real!" He raises his hands in a gesture of defeat. "I see you, little Owl. Isn't that enough? It's all I have. I am an elemental, made for one thing only. Not to be a father. Go back, go back to your human life. The Earl will not hurt you. It is forbidden for him to interfere in humanity."

"He already did it once!"

"He will not hurt you." Jack shakes his head. "And I will be back, by and by, I expect. I will call in on you. Will that be nice? A visit from your . . . from . . ." His glib tone falters, he cannot even say the word. He still doesn't really believe it, I realize, as his troubled eyes look me up and down. Perhaps he thinks it's all some trick. That I'm just here to get him into further trouble.

"It doesn't matter," I whisper to myself, looking at Avery. I've done all I can here. I have to get him home. And I've decided—Jack's coming too, whether he likes it or not. The Royal Court needs to know what the Earl did. I need my life back before I ruin it entirely.

“What is it, little Owl?” he asks, following me as I slide down from the bench onto the rug. I reach for Avery, grabbing his cold hand, and look back at Jack, not speaking, waiting until he’s close enough . . . Then I grab his arm, ignoring a howl of protest, and close my eyes, digging down deep to where the cold comes from—where the *magic* comes from—knowing I’m risking everything. If I use too much I’ll become stuck between two worlds and unable to communicate with either, but Avery’s already halfway there because of me, and Jack is never going to come willingly. There’s nothing else I can do. I close my eyes, see the page of the book in my mind, and will us all back to Mallory.

41

We're not in the apartment.

Before I've even opened my eyes, I know I'm outside. A bitter wind howls through the darkness, and over my head is a thick pattern of interweaving branches. Beneath me the ground is soft, mossy. Avery is curled up beside me, motionless. Somebody's covered us both in leaves. I reach out and touch his cheek: his skin is cold. Deep shadows are scored beneath his eyes and my heart clatters in my chest. He's still far too pale.

"Avery?" My voice is sharp against the silence. He doesn't stir. I put my hand on his chest and feel the steady rise and fall. He's alive—barely. Because of me. I could just bury myself right here and sleep for a year. I don't know how I'll face him. I don't know how I'll face anyone. Suddenly there's a scuffling behind us and then a figure looms over me, a shadow against the night sky, a hand reaching down to me. I shuffle back, letting out a whimper of fear.

"Shh, Owl, it's just me," says Mallory in a whisper, pulling me up out of the shadows. She grabs me in a tight hug. "Thank God you're back."

"Mallory! What happened? Where are we? Where's Jack?"

"Jack?"

"I grabbed him, to bring him back."

In the darkness it's difficult to make out much, but it's clear that Jack isn't here. Mallory has pulled me out to a stretch of level ground, covered in thick, coarse grass. Stunted, tangled trees rise in a mass behind us, blackened limbs twisting and reaching out in all directions. Before us and to either side I can just make out ripples of water, catching the silver light of the waning moon. A mist rolls over the top of everything, adding to the chill. I huddle close to Mallory as she shakes her head, her eyes a little wild.

"I haven't seen Jack," she says.

"What happened, Mall? Why are we here?"

"They came for you," she says. "They wanted you, but you weren't there. . . . They took me instead. I guess they knew you'd find me— "

"They grabbed you? Are you all right? Who was it?"

"I think it was the Earl's men," she whispers. "He was furious when they came back without you. The Lady made them bring me here to keep me away from him. We're on an island in the middle of the lake."

Her eyes go to the far shore, where the Old Druid Wood begins. The mist shifts in a whisper of wind and reveals monstrous figures gathered there, shadows moving among the trees, some of them tall, others flitting between, their movements too fast to be anything human, all of them lit by moon-pale globes nestled into the ground.

"But how . . . how did they grab you, Mall? What about Mom, is she okay?"

"They came in through the window," she says with a shudder. "Never seen anything like it, the way they move, so fast and silent. I didn't have time to shout or anything. Your mom was up in the studio. She can't have heard them. I hardly heard them myself."

"It sounds awful—I'm so sorry, Mallory. I'm so sorry for everything. I don't know what I was doing. I went too far. . . . I've nearly killed Avery, and I still don't know what I'm going to do." I look around, feeling utterly hopeless. "How did you get through the barrier, anyway?" I ask. "I thought humans couldn't get here. . . ."

"It's their spell." She shrugs. "I guess they can turn it off, if they want to. . . . Don't look so panicked, we'll work it out." But her smile is thin and her eyes are full of fear. It must have been terrifying for her to be grabbed like that. I've never seen her look so lost. Usually it's she who has all the answers.

Mallory and I used to fight when we first met. We were four. We liked the same games, but we didn't want to play them in the same way. She's always been a stickler for order and rules. I just ran around like a wild thing, infuriating her when occasionally it went right purely by accident.

"This is the way you do it," she'd say, trying to be patient.

"Why?" I'd demand, drawing extra squares onto the hopscotch so we could do more "danceyish sorts of things."

She'd stick her chin out and give me a withering look. She was good at those, even at four. "Because that's the way you do it!"

"Well, I'm not doing it that way," I'd say, thrusting my own chin out.

And then she'd go and tell on me, or I'd go and tell on her. And the teacher—Mrs. Perrin—would have to explain again the importance of compromise and patience and playing fairly, and we'd listen and nod seriously and then carry on just as before.

She'll always do the right thing, Mallory. There's no

way in the world she'd be in this mess if it weren't for me. She'd never have let herself get involved if it was for anyone but me. But we've spent our lives talking about my need for answers about my father, and that's why she came along for the ride. She's here in spite of everything.

"It'll be all right," I say, drawing closer to her. "They won't hurt us."

"Won't they?" she asks, her voice wobbling. "I don't know what happened while you were with Jack, but the Earl is furious. And he's terrifying, Owl."

We stare out across the lake together, watching as the mist starts to clear and the crowd on the other shore grows.

"Why are you here?" asks a voice behind us. It's a woman's voice, but it sounds like nothing I've heard before. There isn't just one tone to it, it's both deep and high, melodious and stern. My skin flares with shock as we turn to see a small figure break free from the undergrowth, her features hidden beneath a vast, sweeping cloak. She stoops to Avery and gives a tut of disapproval.

"Come, wake, boy," she says. "You're in the land of the living now, better act like it!" She reaches out with a small, wrinkled hand and gives him a sound smack across the face.

Avery coughs and begins to stir, and the woman nods, satisfied, as I breathe a sigh of relief. I want to rush over to him, tell him I'm sorry, see the fire back in his eyes, but there's no chance. The woman turns to Mallory and me, her golden eyes glittering as she takes us in. "What are you two doing here? What is going *on* in this place? Can I not leave it for a moment without everything falling apart? Frozen boys and frightened little girls . . . What is it? What has happened? I cannot be everywhere at once, goodness! Why is it so dark?" She glares around at the island and little starlike pinpricks of golden light break out over the ground around us, spreading over the island and up the trees like a veil, bathing us all in a warm glow.

"That's better," she says, looking satisfied. The tiny lights glimmer in response, almost as if they're alive, and Mallory clutches at me in amazement, her fingers gripping tight.

"Who are you?" I ask, trying to keep my voice steady.

"A good question. The very best sort of question," the woman says, stooping to sit opposite us, raising a hand to lower her hood. "Who am I? Could you tell me who you are so easily? Do you even yet know?"

I gape speechlessly as she grins at us, and I'm fairly sure Mallory is doing the same next to me, which seems to amuse the woman even more. She's tiny and ancient, her skin wrinkled, and yet her presence makes my eyes ache. It's as though the air around her is vibrating. Avery shuffles farther back into the undergrowth as if he's trying to disappear, his eyes wide with warning.

"What is it?" I mouth at him.

"Avery, come and join your friends," says the woman without turning. He flinches and starts to move toward us, his footsteps dragging. "Leave your shame behind," she says, shaking her head as he edges around her, coming finally to sit next to me. "It's quite ridiculous and has no place here." She glances across to the woodland across the water and her expression tightens. "What are they doing *now*?" she asks in a whisper. "What can they be thinking of?"

"They're trying to work out what to do with the 'human stain,'" Mallory says in a clear voice. "That's to say, me and Avery, and Owl too."

Avery starts to sputter beside me. I can't tell whether he's outraged or just surprised. I wonder if he's feeling as muddled as I am. Mallory seems to have no inhibitions, but the woman before us has taken my voice, almost my breath, with her presence.

"And so the Earl condemns his own son," she says heavily.

"He would have to, if he wanted to be rid of Owl," Mallory says. "They're the same, aren't they? Half . . . fay, half human?"

"And they say that is a curse. . . ."

"He says it's forbidden," Mallory says, her voice

hushed. "He says it's all gone too far, and now that I've hung out with them, *I* know all their secrets—"

"He says it is forbidden *by whom*?" cuts in the woman, steel in her voice as she watches Mallory closely.

"By Mother Earth."

The woman flinches as if she's been struck, her aura expanding around her until I can feel it in the air, a warp that stings with fury. "And so they would do this in my name. Destroy life, claim souls, in *my name*?"

"I don't know, I . . . maybe I was wrong . . ." Mallory stutters.

"No," says the woman, shaking her head as she stares at the gathering on the bank of the lake. "I expect you're right." Her voice is still tight with anger, but the warp in the air begins to ease as she watches. "I suppose I should have seen where this was heading. I did not think they would go so far. There are troubles in other parts of the world, troubles these idiots have no notion of. I was busy while they continued this ridiculous war with each other. Now this." Her eyes snap back to me. "And you are at the heart of it all. . . ."

"Who are you?" I whisper. Because it can't really be *her*, can it?

"I have many names," she says. "Avery knows them all, I expect?"

I look at Avery. He's completely transfixed by the

figure before us, his eyes like saucers as he gazes at her. He nods, but doesn't speak, which makes her crooked smile widen.

"Mother Earth, they call me here," she says, standing. She seems to grow as she rises, until she towers above us all, her long white hair catching the moonlight. "Now. It's time to sort all of this out. Where is your father, Owl? Did you not bring him with you?"

"I tried to," I stammer. "I don't think it worked."

"I wonder," she murmurs. "Come on, up with you all. You've had some fine adventures, I'm sure, and that's all very well, but now it's time to fix this. Make us a path, Owl—we must cross. And there's no need to look so sheepish. Any complaint they have about humans and fay mixing is not mine. The world turns, and things change. If there is any constant, it is that. If you weren't so full of childish nonsense I might even be quite proud of you."

42

FABLES & EARTH SPIRITS

Mother Earth

It was everything, and nothing. The world spread out before her, vast and unending. She saw starlight and moonlight there, shadows spread across the land, and then the sun broke over the horizon, the fiery dawn of a new day. And she stood at the edge of it all, bare feet upon desert sand, untethered. Lost.

"You are a brave one," came a woman's voice. A woman's voice, but no woman there. Instead a swoop of white wings before the orange sun, a flurry of feathers and golden eyes that seemed to see straight to the very heart of her.

"Who are you?" the girl whispered to the owl, as it settled before her. "What is this place?"

The powerful wings lifted and spread, and a new brightness shone there for just an instant. When it cleared there stood before her an ancient woman, her golden eyes unblinking.

"This is the dawn," said the woman. "And you may call me Mother Earth."

43

My knees tremble as I step out onto the lake, and for a moment, I'm absolutely convinced I'm just going to sink and they'll have to pull me out like a half-drowned rat. But then I look down and see that my bare feet aren't sinking. They're glittering in the light of the globes, ice stretching out around them.

"Very nice," says Mother Earth. "Now keep it good and strong, Owl—your companions aren't so well-equipped for water walking."

I hold my breath and take another step forward onto a frozen pathway that creaks as it gathers before us. I risk a look back and see Avery pushing Mallory onto the ice, Mother Earth behind them. Mallory looks absolutely petrified and I reach back a hand. "It'll be fine," I whisper, grabbing her and pulling her into line with my footsteps. "Trust me."

"It's not that I don't trust you," she hisses, slithering in my wake. "It's just that I'm starting to wonder if I've gone completely stark raving mad and actually I'm in some sort of asylum and you're all figments of my imagination!"

I can't help but grin as I look back at her. "Well, if you're there, then I'm there with you. Let's go with it for now?"

She nods, and I turn to concentrate on making sure the path of ice is going in the right direction. As the shore gets closer I can make out the figures of those gathered there. The Earl, his towering figure never still as he gestures to those gathered before him. The Lady, who sits on the edge of the shore, her feet still in the lake. The dozens of fay creatures gathered between them. As I watch they're joined by two more figures: the North Wind and the Queen, her pink hair lit by the globes. A shiver runs over me at the idea of facing them.

"Where is Jack?" demands Mother Earth crossly.

"He might not . . . He doesn't really want to . . . uh . . ."

My pace falters, the ice cracking beneath my feet as all my doubts threaten to overwhelm me. It should be reassuring that Mother Earth is with us, but there are so many on the shore, and if my own father won't speak up for me, why should anybody else? What if I'm just leading us all into more danger?

"Doesn't want to come and face his enemies, eh? Always been more for sulking and hiding, that one," Mother Earth says.

Mallory squawks behind me as a layer of water begins to wash over the narrow trail, soaking our feet. I close my eyes in a desperate attempt to get it back under control, and then someone grabs my free hand, a squall of ice hitting me in the face.

"Come, little Owl," says a familiar voice, thick with humor. "You cannot falter here!"

The lake freezes around us with a creaking sound and I open my eyes to see my father standing before me at the start of an incredible, still-developing bridge that sweeps up in front of us and leads to the far shore. Jack's eyes twinkle with laughter as I stare, spellbound, at the shimmering ice structure. Slim white pillars stretch skyward, cutting into the night sky, and pale spirals wink between them, catching starlight and reflecting it down onto a glass-like walkway.

"You came back," I manage feebly.

"I did—though the journey was a little more hair-raising than usual. You need to practice your spells!"

"Jack, it's about time," breaks in Mother Earth. "What have you been doing?"

"The wrong things . . ." he says blithely, bowing to her

and pulling on my hand, leading me forward. "As ever."

Mother Earth grunts as she and the others follow us onto the bridge. "I suggest you start to work on that. There's not only yourself to worry about now, is there?" She looks at me with a wicked gleam in her eye.

"I didn't think it was possible for me," he says in a tight voice.

"You thought the rest of the world would evolve without you? You are as changed as any creature. I did not cast you in stone, Jack."

"No," he says, lowering his eyes for an instant. "I see that. And I'm here now, though I'm afraid I've revealed us. . . . The Lady can always feel my touch. Somehow, little Owl, your own touch had gone by her unnoticed."

"She is more careful than you," says Mother Earth caustically. "A little less showy . . ." She gestures at the bridge as the walkway continues to unfold before us with ever more intricate details: prisms glinting beneath the surface, slender vines curling around the pillars. "And more gentle, too, when she's not half crazed. Perhaps you can learn from each other, if we get through this. . . ."

"If?" I ask, my voice wobbling.

"They are many. We are few."

"But you're . . . you're Mother Earth!"

"We'll see," she says.

I catch Avery's eye as I look back at her. His jaw is

tight with strain, and he's hardly said a word since we've been back, but he does look far better than he did before, so I suppose I should just be grateful for that. He winks as I stare at him but there's no humor in it, only a steely determination. He's about to face down his father for the first time, and even with Jack and Mother Earth on our side he looks like he wishes the world would just swallow him up instead.

I turn back to Jack as the Lady begins to shout in the distance, as the strange figures all turn to look at us.

"Look what you've got us all into, little Owl," Jack says, not looking back at me. "At least your boy has come through unscathed. . . ." His voice is full of energy, his footsteps brisk along the ice.

He's looking forward to this fight.

"I'll leave you all to it, then," Mother Earth says as we come within clear view of the shore, which is bustling with activity. "You'll have to fight for yourselves, you know."

"Why?" asks Mallory.

"I cannot be here to fight all your battles. There are many things that call for my attention," she says. "I'll be watching, don't you worry. And I'll back you up if the need is dire. It is better if you can do this yourselves."

"Come, then," says Jack. "We can face down the Earl,

can we not, Avery? Are you sure you stand on the right side of this? Can you do it?"

"Let's just get on with it," says Avery in a strained voice.

"So, so," says Jack. "Time for action."

I'm still watching Mother Earth as she changes. Her figure seems to fold into shadow. That buzz in the air around her becomes deafening for just a split second, before the shadow unfurls once more, quickly revealing the shape of an owl. White wings spread as she lifts into the air, powerful muscles contracting as she rises, higher and higher.

"Owl!" Mallory says. "What are you doing?"

I turn to her, to find them all watching me. "What? Didn't you see . . ."

"See what?" asks Jack. "Focus now, little Owl. We will need to work together here." He peers around me. "She's gone already. Well, we must make the best of it, yes?"

I nod, dry-mouthed, looking from one to the other of them. Quizzical faces peer back at me. None of them saw her turn into an owl. Does anyone know that's her other form? Was it she who rescued me from the Green Man when I came to the Royal Court the first time? Was it she who defended me against the wolves? Is she the one who comforted my mother, who knew that I would exist before anyone else did? Was she the one who spoke to me in my room, calling on me to reveal the truth about the Earl's manipulations?

"Jack!" The North Wind's booming voice comes, interrupting my thoughts as he blows a blizzard of snow onto the bridge. "We can all see you. Now, come and explain yourself to this ridiculous flapping Earl. He can hardly contain himself!"

The globe-like lights that lend their glow to the Royal Court are actually some kind of mushroom, I've worked out. I've worked it out because I've been staring resolutely at them for the last ten minutes. They're very beautiful, in an alien sort of way.

I think I should probably be doing something, only I'm not sure what. I'm standing between Mallory and Avery in the shadow of the Green Man. We've been put here while debate rages on what to do with us. Jack is passionate as he argues on our behalf, defending himself and the "human stain" he has brought with him. He seems reluctant to call out the Earl on his part in creating all this trouble, but I think he's enjoying the thrust and parry of hot, hard words. My eyes keep flicking to Avery as I listen, and every so often I open my mouth to speak to him, to say I'm sorry, to let him know how grateful I am for everything, but he's silent and dark-eyed, watching with an intensity that I don't dare to interrupt. He won't want to hear it, anyway. He risked his life to save mine, and I nearly killed him for it. What can I possibly say after that?

The North Wind is standing with Jack, his large form reverberating with power, a bubbling flurry of activity all around him. He was the one to welcome us as we sidled onto the shore.

"Ahh, little one," he whispered with a wink at me as he pulled me forward onto solid ground, his huge hands dwarfing mine. "I am glad to see you. Now, come, let's sort this out. I don't care for all this fussing. It gets in the way of the game."

I looked nervously at the hordes of fay creatures clustered in the trees, their excited chatter making the air ring, then the Earl stepped up, towering over all of us, his skin shining in the pale light. He has Avery's coloring, and his facial features aren't all that different, but there's a coldness, a cruelty there that I've never seen on Avery's face. I couldn't help but look at Avery as his father folded his arms, glaring down at us. I could see the movement in his neck as he swallowed, the throb of the pulse in his temple as he forced himself to meet the Earl's eyes.

"Father," he said in a cool voice that belied the tense curl of his fists.

The Earl's hard eyes widened for a second before he turned his glare to Jack.

"What do you do here, Jack?" he asked. "The Royal Court's decision was final, at least for this season. You have no place here. And that you have descended upon us with this . . . this collection of little *monsters* is beyond what I'd have expected, even from you!"

"Are you not delighted that I have broken the rules?" Jack demanded. "Surely this plays perfectly into your character assassination of me. This has been a long time coming, has it not?"

The Earl paled as Jack hinted at what he knew, but before either of them could continue, the Lady called out, her voice clear and firm.

"We are in the Royal Court—this is not the place for idle threats and accusations," she said. "Come, Jack. Leave your companions and let us deal with this properly."

"My companions have their own voices," Jack said coolly.

"And perhaps they will be heard. There are questions that only you can answer, however, and those are the most pressing. . . ."

"We need to go and tell them the truth!" I say now, watching as the argument rages backward and forward, never seeming to get anywhere. The Queen of May is clearly on the Earl's side, her soft features twisted into something dreadful with the malice she has for Jack.

Their battle is eternal, I realize as I watch them. Every year, the same thing, as she tries to break through winter with spring's new life. I pull away from the others as the conversation gets more heated, the Earl towering over my father, but the Green Man whips a branch around my waist before I can get any further.

"Stop that!" I shout. "Let me go!"

"Child, calm yourself," he says in his deep, gentle voice. I look up into his gnarled face and see endless patience there. Who knows what it would take to change his mind about anything?

"They're just fighting. They're not changing anything!" I cry.

"And how will *you* change their minds?"

"I'll tell the truth," I say, gritting my teeth and staring him in the eye.

"Very well," he says with laughter in his voice, "but first you must get away from me. . . ."

"The Earl did this," I tell him desperately. "He sent my mother to Jack. He arranged all of it!"

"So you say!" the Green Man says, genuine surprise on his face as he looks back to the bickering figures. "I suppose he was seeking his revenge . . ."

"Revenge for what?" Avery asks now. "Why *is* he so mad at Jack?"

"They were angry at each other," the Green Man

replies, his leaves rustling as he shrugs. "The Earl of October wanted his power to last until midwinter—said it was only fair that he have his season uninterrupted by Jack's play. Jack said winter has no such rules. He said the Earl's very name spoke of his limitations—Earl only for October, only for one month. The Earl was furious, accused Jack of meddling with his season. Jack got more and more wild—bringing frosts as early as September, even, and late, too, so that he was treading on the Queen of May's toes. She is the real power behind the Earl, you know," he muses, watching them as if he's forgotten we're there. "I suppose they orchestrated this little outrage together."

"And that's it?" I interrupt, a bit stung at being referred to as a "little outrage." "That's what this is all about?"

"What else is there?" he asks, his gaze returning to me. "When you exist only for one reason, and another interferes with that, there is no more powerful incentive for rage."

44

"We have to help," I whisper to Avery and Mallory, while the Green Man's attention is once more drawn to the argument going on in the clearing by the lake. "Jack's outnumbered, isn't he?"

Avery shrugs, his expression stony. "The Lady won't intercede for him—she never does. The Queen of May and the Earl against Jack and the North Wind . . . Not sure who'd win that."

"But all the . . . all the sprites and the goblins are on the Earl's side. Can't you see?" We peer out at the gathering from the Green Man's branches. "They think Jack's working against nature's harmony or something."

"He kind of does do that," Avery says.

"But isn't that the point? Nature isn't all daisies and rainbows, is it?"

"No, it isn't," says Mallory. "There's danger, unpredictability . . . That's what makes it what it is." Avery looks down at her, surprised. "What?" she demands hotly. "Just because I'm a human *stain* doesn't mean I don't care about it. I'm as much a part of the world as you are, y'know." She sticks her chin out and Avery grins, shaking his head.

"Anyway," I say. "The fact is that the Earl cheated when he tried to get Jack removed. He's planned this for years. We should be calling him out on that."

Before I can say anything else, Avery strides out of the Green Man's shelter, summoning a fierce wind that tosses branches and leaves out of his way. I grab Mallory and follow him as he heads straight for the Royal Court, hardly hearing the surprised bellow behind us.

"Boy, get back to your hiding place!" roars the Earl when he sees Avery approaching. "I will deal with you later!" He moves toward Avery, but Jack steps smoothly between them, pushing Avery protectively behind him with one arm.

"What are you afraid of now, Earl?" he demands, humor still in his voice. "What scandal has your son got up his sleeve?"

"Ridiculous!" blusters the Earl, his mottled skin darkening, long limbs restless with agitation. The Queen of May stands strong by his side. Her green eyes are fierce as she glances from Jack to Avery, and then to Mallory and me, and the goblins show their teeth, but there's instant confusion among the sprites and the fairies. They draw away from the Earl, talking in low whispers among themselves. From what I can make out, the Earl's attitude toward Avery is as troubling for them as it is for me.

"Is it ridiculous, Father?" Avery says in a low voice, his eyes finally meeting the Earl's. "Do you really think I'd stand here against you without good reason?"

"Reason?" The Earl chokes. "You have very little of reason, boy. Your mother saw to that. She was too weak for this world, and you are touched by the same madness!"

He knows, I realize. He knows that we have got to the bottom of it. He knows that if he allows us to speak, if he allows the Royal Court to really hear us, *he's* the one who will be in disgrace.

"Just say it," I whisper, edging up to Avery, sliding my fingers between his, a huge surge of relief rushing through me when he clenches my hand tight and takes a deep breath.

"You are in league with *her*! Has she turned you further?" the Earl snarls, coming closer. I catch a whiff of his scent: warm and copper bright, but beneath it, the reek of decay. The Queen of May stares at me and I flinch. Her eyes are wide and they take in every part of me, seem to see everything I am, everything I ever might be. They're formidable together, his rage and her quiet determination steering everything. Avery takes his hand from mine and stands straighter, but it's as though we're caught in their spell. Neither of us can say what we had intended.

"You did this!" chimes Mallory's voice. She takes a step forward, tiny before the Earl yet so fearless. My heart races and I *will* myself to move, to stand by her, but I cannot move a muscle. The Queen's gaze has me trapped.

Mallory folds her arms in a gesture I recognize well. She's not going to back down now. I've never been so proud, or so terrified for her. The Earl looms over her, his face a picture of shock and indignation, and the whole Royal Court waits, listening, mesmerized by the standoff between them.

"You sent Owl's mother to Jack by giving your power to the spell she cast. You had them create Owl—all so you could discredit Jack, so that you could send him away!"

Nothing moves. Not even the pale mushroom globes seem to flicker as Mallory's words ricochet through the Royal Court. It's as though she's set off an explosion: a silent, deadly bomb that has rocked the very core of this reality for a split second.

"No!" breathes the Lady finally. She has been silent throughout, watching it all with a luminous grace that seemed completely impenetrable. That, now, is gone. Her fists clench with fury as she looks from Mallory to the Earl and sees the flicker of truth in his eyes before he has time to gather himself. The Queen of May smoothly steps away from him, as if she had nothing to do with it all, as the owl glides in to land on the Lady's shoulder, and I find I can move once more.

I race to Mallory, putting my arm through hers, standing with her against the towering rage I see building in the Earl's every breath. He looks around at the gathered crowd, which has moved away from him, almost on instinct. He is careful not to look in the direction of the Queen of May, and I wonder what hold she has over him, and whether he'll take the heat for it all. I *know* she played a part in it.

Jack and the North Wind come to stand beside Mallory and me, and the Earl is alone now before us.

"What is this?" he demands, hot panic in his voice. "Avery!"

"Yes?" Avery breaks through us to stand in front of his father.

"What madness have you been spreading? I should have left you in that hovel. I should have left you to die with your deranged mother. I should *never* have acknowledged you, given you shelter here, given you a place as my *son*!" Spittle flies as he rants, desperation clinging to every syllable. "This is *lies*! Why would I seek to create more of your kind, twisted by the weaknesses of humanity? Why would I give the power of the elements to a human child? What is this that you have cooked up between you? Is it Jack's doing? Did he conspire to have you lie before me?"

Avery braces himself against his father's venom, and I want to intervene, I want to roar at the Earl, to run up and push him bodily away from his son, and I can see that Mallory feels the same—but we cannot. Jack and the North Wind have their hands on our arms. Their eyes hold a world of warning.

"Why?" I whisper desperately.

"This is Avery's fight," Jack whispers back. "Don't you think he has earned it, after all this time?"

"I heard you," Avery says, breathing hard. "You couldn't contain yourself—you were so pleased at what you had achieved. It didn't matter to you that you were destroying what Mother Earth had put in place, that you burdened Owl with the impossible job of her father. You were rid of him. You thought you'd have an easy ride, that autumn would blend with spring. Did you think of what that would do to the world? Or were you so besotted with *her*—" he looks at the Queen of May, who watches serenely, apparently completely unfazed by his words "—that you forgot why *you* were here, what any of this is for? Would you really stand and call me a liar, when you know that I am not? Doesn't it mean anything to you that I am . . . that I . . ."

His voice breaks off and suddenly I feel something building in the air. Something that stings and burns with some kind of frantic rage. Frowning, I look from the Earl to the Queen. And I see it there, in her eyes. Furious and full of spite, she has charged the air with her power: static that gathers thickly around her, just waiting to be let loose. I look to Jack and see that he can feel it, too—he just hasn't figured out where it's coming from. I try to indicate the Queen with my eyes, but he's not looking. He's watching the Earl.

"What say you, old friend?" he asks him, his voice gentle, almost conciliatory. "Can you really deny it, before all of us gathered here? I have been at fault myself, if that is of comfort. I should have seen the truth straight away. Owl *is* my daughter. She bears *my* power and *her* humanity with a wisdom I have spent thousands of years chasing. Would you not say the same of your son?"

The Earl looks from Avery to Jack, and then at me, as the crowd around us begins to stir once more, everyone wide-eyed and whispering. His body is taut with rage and the Queen's eyes glow. He is her weapon, I realize. He is the spark.

"*MONSTERS!*" he howls. The Queen lays a hand on

his arm as if to placate him, but I see the jolt of her power as it connects with his, and, eyes burning, he strikes out at Avery. My skin freezes as static rushes toward him and he doesn't move. He doesn't see the electricity coming his way. Or he doesn't care. Fear slams through my body. My heartbeat is a siren in my blood and I don't think, I just throw myself in front of him, raising my arm against the scalding wind and reaching desperately for my power as electricity leaps at me.

I brace myself for the hit, closing my eyes, every nerve in my body tingling with energy—then there's a *whump* of silence all around me. My hair stands on end, but it doesn't hurt. After a moment I realize I'm still breathing, still standing. I open my eyes, but I can't see anything, can't hear anything. A thick white mist blooms in the air before me. Particles of frost slowly drift to the ground. There's no trace of the static electricity.

What happened? I blink, my mind reeling, and slowly the mist begins to clear. The Earl is stationary before me, his face frozen with frustration, literally frozen: his skin ice blue, his hair plastered in frost, icicles dripping from his outstretched limbs. His eyes are fixed on me, unblinking.

"Couldn't have done *that* better myself!" shouts Jack, jumping beside me as Mallory looks on with worried eyes, the North Wind silent beside her. The Queen of

May moves further back, something like fear in her gaze as she stares from Jack to me.

"What did you do?" Avery hisses in my ear, grabbing my arm tight. "Have you killed him?"

"I don't know," I manage past a lump in my throat, staring at the unmoving Earl. "I'm sorry, I didn't mean to . . . Avery, I swear!" I turn to Jack, who marches up to the Earl and flicks him on the nose. There's no reaction. It's as though he's a statue.

"He'll be fine," Jack sighs eventually. "You hit back, defended yourself with your power. He just needs a good thaw. You can't kill him so easily as that, sadly. If it were possible, I'd have done it a long time ago. . . ."

Though I know—I know from the way he intervened with Avery—that he'd never do that.

"Jack!" thunders a multilayered voice behind us. "That's quite enough." The figure of Mother Earth coalesces before us in a magical moment of pale, blurred wings and shifting robes, for an instant almost too bright to see. A new silence descends upon the whole Royal Court, every figure frozen in place as they turn to see her lined face, taut with rage. "This isn't a game. You are hurting real people. Look at these children who have had to fight for their lives just because of some petty dispute!" She marches up to the Earl and gives him a slap on the shoulder. Instantly the ice falls away from him and he awakens with a cough. "You!" Mother Earth says. "What were you thinking to aim your rage at your only son? What is this crusade against humanity? Were you put here to harm life, to endanger nature's work? What say you?"

The Earl's eyes are like caverns as he stares at Mother Earth. He splutters as he tries to find the words.

"I sought to conserve our . . . our legacy," he manages after a long moment, bowing his head before Mother Earth.

"Your legacy!" She looks like she'd like to slap him again. "What has happened to you all?" She looks around at her Royal Court. At the sprites, who have watched without saying a word. At the Lady of the Lake, who has sat mute throughout the fight. At the Queen of May, whose skin is flushed. "I am ashamed of you. Thousands of years of work it has taken to achieve harmony. You were its guardians! Did you think you ruled this earth? No! You are servants to all who dwell here. It is your *job* to protect and to nurture. None of you has remembered what you fight for, what you are preserving. Even having created your own *children*, you fail to see the beauty in them, the frailty and the power they balance." She rounds on them one by one. "Jack! You are too proud, too wild. It is in your nature to be flighty, but you are not a power unbridled, you may not step outside your bounds. And you!" She turns to the Earl. "This fixation on 'human stains' and your own sense of importance is absurd. It goes against everything I ever worked to achieve. And as for you . . ." She turns to the Queen of May, her voice simmering.

"Yes," says the Queen calmly, stepping forward. "What of me? What have you to say that you think I will abide by? You forget that *you* are the head of this Royal Court. Everything that we are, everything that we have become, is because of you. If we have evolved, that was because you allowed it!"

Mother Earth narrows her eyes and a ripple of tension rolls through the Royal Court, crowds huddling tight together, eyes all fixed on her. "Yes," she says eventually, the globe lights dimming, even the moon seeming to pale as her anger throbs in the air around us. "Yes, I have allowed it. I gave you freedom with your responsibility. I gave you choices, companionship. I sought to create harmony. . . ." Her voice dwindles as the entire Royal Court hangs on every word. "Truly, I thought you would see sense before it came to this. Clearly I should have held the reins tighter. Go now, little queen. Go and rest until your season is upon us. I will think on this while you are incapacitated." She stretches her arm out in the Queen's direction, fingers spread wide, and the Queen flinches, caught up and powerless, slowly losing form until all that remains is the hint of a spring breeze. "And you, Earl, your time is also past for this year. Begone!" She makes the same motion, and the Earl flings his arms up as if to protect himself, but it is no defense. In an instant he is nothing but a swirl of brittle, autumn leaves that slowly drifts to the ground.

"As for the rest of you," she says, her eyes luminous as she turns to take in the whole Royal Court, her voice ringing out. "This is not over. You have allowed these two to wield more power than I ever gave them. You will know peace for as long as winter lasts, but they will be back, and it is up to you to fight them. I will not intervene again. I cannot be here to mother you all of the time!"

"We understand," says the Lady of the Lake, stepping regally onto the shore, silver water pouring off her as she comes toward Mother Earth. She bows deeply, and the rest of the Royal Court follow in one fluid motion, Jack and the North Wind joining them, Avery and I, and even Mallory, making our own clumsy efforts.

"Well, I should think so," says Mother Earth with a shake of her head.

45

I am so exhausted that the world seems to slow with it, everything heavy, muted. I watch as Avery is taken to one side by the Lady of the Lake, her eyes concerned at his pallor. He doesn't look back at me as he argues with her, trying to fend off her concern in typical Avery style. He probably blames me for getting his father ousted, or for nearly killing him.

I'll never forget how still he was.

I'll never get over what I nearly did.

Mallory is talking animatedly to the Green Man, and my father is being lectured by Mother Earth, who keeps gesturing to the bridge over the lake as if it's a symbol of everything he shouldn't be doing. He's nodding and bowing and very nearly wringing his hands, and slowly the bridge begins to melt, falling away into the water, but there's still a glint of pride in his eye and he doesn't look in the slightest bit chastened. He is so different here, it's almost as if he's playing up to his reputation. I know now, from how he was in his own world, that he cares more than he lets on.

Thousands of sprites and fairies flit from place to place, their every movement full of excitement, tiny rainbows breaking out around them as the sun begins to rise. I look at Avery once more, and for an instant I think I can see right through him, but when I blink and look again he's just himself, a boy with a bit of the unusual about him, still reluctantly being inspected by the Lady. He shrugs away from her as she fusses, but I can see he likes it really—already his eyes are less haunted. It makes me think of Mom, which sends a little pang through me.

"Owl," says Mallory, coming up to me, her face shining. "You did it!"

"*You* did it," I say with a smile, as my knees turn rubbery. I lean into her. "I couldn't find my voice. It was you who did it!"

"Perhaps being a human stain counts for something," she says, smiling back. "But it was incredible, what you did to the Earl. Are you okay? Are you feeling solid?"

I hesitate for a moment, distracted by the complete craziness of such a question.

"I think so," I say, looking down at myself. "Don't I look solid?"

"You do," she says. "You look absolutely Owl-like, as ever. It'll be all right, Owl. They're gone."

"For now," I say.

"And your father is here, and he's proud of you," she adds, brushing past the awkward moment. "I could tell he was, Owl, and so he can teach you, can't he, how to use your power without getting caught between worlds?"

"I suppose so," I say. "I just . . . uh!" I pull her down to sit with me. "It's all so crazy. Tell me something normal. Did I miss anything the last couple of days?"

Mallory laughs at me, shaking her head. "Nothing to compete with all of this. I did talk to Dad last night, before everything else happened."

"And?"

"It was okay," she says. "He's going to take me out this weekend so we can talk properly so that's—" Her phone buzzes, cutting her off. She takes it out of her pocket, looks at the screen, and flushes bright red.

"What is it?"

"Nothing," she says, tucking the phone hurriedly back into her pocket.

"Mallory!"

"What?"

"You can't not tell me! I thought we told each other

everything. I told you all my stuff!" I gesture around us at the fay folk. "I've shared *everything*!"

"Hah!" She grins. "But you're not allowed to laugh. Or say anything funny."

"Okay," I promise, pretty sure there's nothing funny in me right now, anyway.

"It was Conor," she says, unable to hide a little smile. "He . . . um . . . he asked if we could go out sometime—"

"A-ha!" I crow. "I knew it! What are you going to say?"

"Don't know," she says with a toss of her head, avoiding my eye. I stare at her. "Oh, fine!" She sighs dramatically. "I'll *probably* say yes. What about you?"

"Me? I don't think Conor's interested in me."

"Ha—I meant about everything else. Avery, for example."

"I don't know what's going to happen there. I suppose it depends if he can get past the fact that I nearly froze him to death," I say, my eyes going to him. There's a little pull in my chest as I watch him, a little shiver that has nothing to do with frost. I hope he can forgive me. I can't quite imagine being without him now. "*Anyway*," I rush on, "I have other things to focus on too. . . ."

I look at Jack, who has finished being lectured and is staring openly at Mallory and me. He winks and comes toward us.

"Little Owl," he says. "You did well out there. Will you come out to play this evening? You said you wanted to learn. . . ."

"Maybe tomorrow," I say, scrambling up, and very grateful that Mallory is there to hang on to. "I've been busy, remember?"

"Ah, yes. Filling in, risking your life for the art of it . . . Good girl, good girl." He pats me on the shoulder, his eyes sparkling. "Then tomorrow. North Wind!" he yells, turning to the North Wind. "Time for a little sparring before full daylight is upon us?"

The North Wind flicks a sidelong look at Mother Earth, who averts her eyes, pretending she hasn't heard. Then he strides toward us, grinning, tossing the air around him as he comes. "Why, yes, Jack," he says, blowing us all back in his enthusiasm. "I mean to say, within reason," he adds, clearing his throat as he looks at Mallory and me. "As ever . . ."

Mallory is enchanted by the excited sprites. They have come up to us, nervously at first, and then in their droves, while fairies watch on from their branches. My eyes are dry and sore. I cannot keep up with their fast-paced chatter, though Mallory seems to be in her element, her usually sober brown eyes alight with the magic of it all. I draw away from them, my head pounding, and find a patch of moss beneath the trees, sitting with my back up against one of the trunks as the burning white sun falls from the sky, fluttering its wings as it comes to land.

The owl.

"It was you. . . ." I manage, as she shudders and breaks apart in front of me, only to appear as Mother Earth once more. "All along, you were there, with Mom, in my room. . . ."

"It was me." She nods. "Did you think you were alone in this? I have watched over you always. You are my namesake. You are destined for even greater things than this, if only you can control yourself. . . ."

I flinch at the stern tone, knowing I deserve that, and more.

"Jack has much to teach you," she says. "But for now it's time for home. Your mother is worried, and you've been lying to her."

Oh, no. I'm going to be in so much trouble. What will I tell her? How long will she ground me for this time?

"But will I be stuck between worlds?" I ask, trying to delay reality a little longer. "Will Avery? What I did to him . . . Will he be all right? What will happen to us all, when *they* return?"

"Ah." She flicks a hand at me. "You take on too much. Not everything that has happened was down to you, and you have done your best, as has Avery. He'll be fine. And he'll forgive you, you know. The harder thing will be to forgive yourself. If you'll take advice from an old woman, do it. Life's too short, even here, to hold on to regret. I've put Avery under the protection of the Green Man and the Lady. They've been more parents than his own have ever been anyway. And you've both shown balance in what you did here today. You have compassion and a rather human ability for loyalty and friendship. I'm not saying it will be easy or safe—you must always work on your strength, both as elemental and human. . . ."

I nod, looking across at Avery. He catches my eye, and though he's still too pale, and though I may never quite forgive myself for everything I've done, he twists one corner of his mouth in a trademark Avery smile and my heart lifts, because it says everything. It says there is hope, which is probably more than I deserve. I don't know what it'll be like tomorrow, whether he'll even come back to school, but I know that somehow, somehow I can fix it. And it matters. *He* matters. Without him and Mallory, I'd have been lost, and so would Jack—perhaps even the whole Royal Court, in time.

"What about Jack?" I ask, when Avery has been drawn into a clumsy hug by the Green Man. "Will he change, after what you said? Will he be . . ." I can't bring myself to finish the sentence. *Will he be a father?*

"Jack will be at his work," she says, watching him

charge off with the North Wind with a shake of her head. They push and shove at each other, tripping and laughing and spinning little flurries of ice between them as they go. "He will guide you in your power. You must not expect too much of him. Much of what you need to do comes from within. Control, balance: only you can master those for yourself. But he came back because of you, I am sure of that. Your existence has changed him, helped him to remember what I taught him so long ago about how precious this life is, that what he is doing is worthwhile. He had lost that faith. I expect he will *try* to be a father, though he'll never be quite what you imagined."

"He'll try?"

"In all sorts of strange and wonderful ways, if I know Jack at all," she says drily. "Now. Home with you, little Owl. I'll not be far. . . ."

46

Mom is not incandescent with rage. She is not jumping up and down shouting at me, grounding me until the end of time.

I wish she was.

Instead she's watching me, watching me, watching me, as if she hasn't seen me for a hundred years. As if she thought she'd never see me again. And it really hurts that I've made her so afraid. It hurts so much that I haven't got the voice to speak, or the strength to give her the hug she needs. I just loiter in the hallway, my back against the front door, while she leans against the adjacent wall, breathing, watching.

I've never known her so silent.

After a while I find the strength to look her in the eye, and then it's all a bit of a mess of crying and snorting and sort of laughing, sort of wailing, and she rushes over and puts her arms around me, bracelets jangling, soft wool cardigan sending fluff up my nose, and I breathe in the warm scent of her and it's as though I haven't been warm, haven't been safe, for so long I'd forgotten what it felt like.

"I'm so angry with you," she says breathlessly as she steps back, a wobbly smile on her face. "I didn't know what to think. The window was open. The room was like a winter wonderland, everything frozen, so beautiful and so cold. . . . And I called Mallory's mother to see if you were there and she was gone too, and I didn't know whether that was better or worse, though she has more sense than you so I supposed it was probably better, but still . . . you must tell me, Owl." Her face grows serious. "You will tell me, won't you? And you won't lie and tell me it was all about a boy, because you . . . you smell of your father's home. And I have been so afraid. And I have waited so long."

"I'll tell you," I say through the lump in my throat. "I'm sorry. I'm so sorry for making you so scared."

And then there's more hugging and fluff up my nose. And then we collect ourselves and trail down to the kitchen, and Mom makes jasmine tea in the cups with the dragons chasing their tails, and I raid the fridge, and we eat a very strange breakfast of hummus and leftover pasta and some of those terrible seed cookies. And we do it all in silence because neither of us can find the words to start until, finally, when the tea has curled down to my belly and warmed my blood, I find the obvious place to begin.

"I found Jack. . . ."

ACKNOWLEDGMENTS

Thank you to my amazing agent, Amber Caraveo, for seeing the potential both in me and in Owl, and steering us in the right direction with such passion and kindness. Thank you to my wonderful UK editors Rachel and Lucy at Macmillan, for taking us in and sharing your wisdom and care. And thank you to Katherine Tegen Books, and especially to editors Kelsey and Rebecca, for giving Owl a home in the United States and for making *The Lost Frost Girl* such a thing of beauty.

Thank you to Richard Kerridge, Mimi Thebo, and everyone else at the Bath Spa MA in creative writing, for taking a punt on me and helping me to recognize that perhaps a dream really *could* become a reality.

Thank you to all of my friends: to Verity, Caroline, Sam, and Nikki for listening to my wild tales and putting up with the occasional lapse in manners when I've been distracted by other worlds or had to check my email for the millionth time; to Tannith, Ken, Harriet, and to Lu Hersey for reading and listening and always encouraging; to Emma Smith-Barton for gentle insistence that, yes, this was indeed possible and for the timely advice that made all the difference; and to Aviva Epstein, my very own Mallory, for many, *many* things but especially for giving the Earl of October his title!

A special BIG thank-you to my family: to Lee, Theia, Aubrey, and Sasha for putting up with all the muddles I found myself in along the way and for putting up with me in general. No matter how much I write I will never be able to express quite what a joy and a privilege it is to have you all in my life.

Thank you to Judith and to Charles, whose quiet words mean much. And to my sister Hannah, and to Dan, and to Martin, who took the time to tell me he was proud of me when there was precious little time left.

Finally, a very special thank-you to my lovely Mum, Helen, for instilling in me a love of books, for knowing what I was capable of long before I did, and for showing me, over and over again, what true strength really looks like. And to my brilliant little brother, Matt, who, if we believed in deserving, deserved so very much more. Your determination humbles me still and will ever inspire me.